THE INNOCENT CHILDREN

A NOVEL BY

D1710234

PETER C. BRADBURY

COPYRIGHT: PETER C. BRADBURY
2013

All characters portrayed in this novel are entirely fictitious. This book is a work of fiction. Names, characters, businesses, organizations, places, events, and incidents are either the author's imagination or are used fictitiously. Any resemblance to actual persons, living or dead, events, or locales are entirely coincidental.

THIS NOVEL IS DEDICATED TO THE VERY FINE MEN AND WOMEN OF THE FBI's CIVIL RIGHTS UNIT and VIOLENT CRIMES AGAINST CHILDREN UNIT.

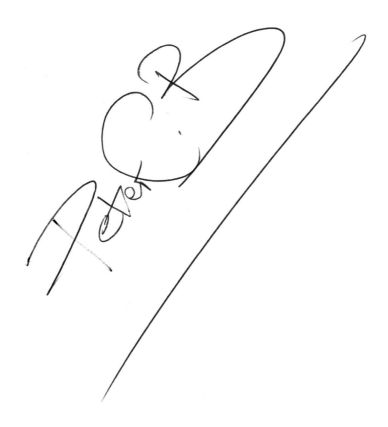

Human trafficking, which is the modern name for slavery, is a huge business generating upwards of 50 billion dollars a year worldwide. In the USA it is estimated that approximately 18,000 people are trafficked into the country each year, half of whom are children. There are also over 1 and half million runaway children every year, 70% of whom end up in the sex trade. Slaves are used for labor, domestic servitude, but mainly for sex, especially the female children. The average age of these children is eleven.

CHAPTER 1

Nobody witnessed the white Ford cargo van as it obeyed the traffic laws and made its way along Brentwood Blvd., in the town of the same name.

This wasn't the Brentwood in the suburbs of Los Angeles that was made famous by O.J. Simpson. This was a small town in the East Bay of San Francisco, filled with fruit farms that invited people to pick their own every summer, and corn fields that the town held an annual festival for.

No one was around as the van proceeded on its route. It was after all, only three thirty in the morning on a weekday, so there were no pedestrians, just an occasional tractor trailer making its way to the docks in Oakland.

As the van passed through the green light at the junction with Sand Creek Road, not slowing down, the side door opened and a woman was thrown out of it, hitting the pavement hard and making her roll several yards. No sooner had she been tossed out, the side door closed and the van continued on as if nothing had happened.

It was almost another hour before a perplexed truck driver who'd stopped for a red light, decided to investigate the unmoving bundle at the side of the road. After moving through the intersection, he parked up his trailer and slowly walked back, not realizing what it was until he was almost upon it.

"Oh fuck," he exclaimed to the empty sidewalk, as he saw it was a long haired brunette, curled into a ball, and she wasn't moving or making any noise.

"Oh fuck," he repeated as he got very close to her, afraid of touching her. What he could see of her wasn't pretty. She had cuts and scrape marks, blood and bruises. The driver didn't know she'd been thrown from a moving vehicle, but she looked to be badly beaten up as he looked for signs of life and called 911.

The 911 responder made him check her for a pulse after she got his name and location, and his hand shook as he felt her right wrist. Her wrist was limp but he thought he detected a faint pulse. He hoped so. He didn't want to be someone who found a dead woman.

The sirens were audible very quickly. The driver wasn't aware that a paramedic station was situated very close to the location, and the police weren't far behind along with a fire truck. The responder had sent everyone.

The medics arrived first and moved in quickly, asking questions that the driver couldn't answer, giving the woman oxygen as they checked her out. Then the police arrived, two patrol cars, and the cops asked questions as the woman had protected splint pads applied to various parts of her body, along with a neck brace, and a drip.

When one of the cops asked the paramedics how she was, they replied that she was in a very bad way as they loaded her into their van and sped away, lights flashing, but no siren on the quiet streets.

As the truck driver was asked yet more questions, a couple of the cops shone their flashlights on the pavement, and when one of them seemed to find something, he called his colleague over who looked at whatever it was, and then they sectioned it off with crime tape.

Yet another cop arrived on the scene, and he looked over the truck driver's cab with his flashlight, as the policeman who'd been asking questions, took the driver's license to his car to check it out.

It wasn't until a couple of crime scene personnel arrived and began putting numbered cards on the pavement, that the truck driver was allowed to leave after talking to a detective who had arrived. He saw the camera flashes and crime scene people in his side mirror as he started the truck up and pulled away, so glad that the woman was still alive.

Despite the efforts of half a dozen medical staff, she never made it out of the emergency room.

Once the autopsy was completed, it was determined that she died from blunt force trauma to her brain after being thrown, or falling, from a moving vehicle. The coroner also determined that she was approximately just twenty five years of age, and she had severe lacerations to most of her body, but not that would cause her death. She had cocaine in her system and needle marks, broken bones from the fall, facial damage, and bruises that were caused during and before the fall, both on her face and on her body. Despite being only in her mid-twenties, she had the characteristics of someone much older with the bodily abuses.

The woman had no identity, her fingerprints had no match, nor was she carrying anything to shed any light on who she was. Not even a tattoo. Her DNA had been sent for comparison, as had her bite for dental records. Unless an I.D. was made from one of them, she would be a Jane Doe.

Jane Doe also had syphilis. It hadn't been treated and she was slowly dying from it, but it was not the cause of her death. Her vagina and anal passageway had been severely abused from a very young age, perhaps as young as eight. The vagina had been so ravaged over time that she would never have been able to have children, and her anal passageway was also damaged and very enlarged.

The Coroner's opinion was that she'd been raped repeatedly from a very young age, and had probably been working as a prostitute for the last few years. Once she contracted the STD, she either had to be treated or discarded once the disease got hold, and as she hadn't had any medication from what he could tell, she was dismissed.

Jane Doe had been a sex slave, and as soon as she was of no further use, she was thrown out with the garbage.

CHAPTER 2

Like many twelve year old girls, Ashley thought she was practically an adult and wanted her family to treat her like one. She and her friends were always complaining to one another about their stupid parents putting locks on their computers and televisions, preventing them from seeing the most interesting websites and programs. It was so unfair.

Then the parents would go on about their grades, homework, when they had to be home, how to dress, that boys were only after one thing, to be nicer to the brat of a younger brother, to eat properly, to get off the phone, do their chores, keep their rooms neat. It was a never ending list of do's and don't's, and Ashley and her friends on Facebook and twitter were fed up of it.

Ashley was a very pretty girl, long blonde hair that was half way down her back, parted in the middle of her head, straight and uncurled. Her features got her a lot of boy interest that she didn't deter, but she wanted her breasts to grow to attract the older boys. Ashley played soccer at school. It was her favorite sport along with swimming and softball, and it kept her trim. She'd just been through puberty which had been 'totally' embarrassing to her, not helped by the teasing of her two brothers.

Her older brother, Greg, was usually okay, but she didn't like her friends flirting with him when they came over. Not that he was interested in any of them, but he did like the attention. Her younger brother, Will, was just a pain. Always telling on her to Mom and Dad, pretending he'd been hit by her, spying on her, and listening when she was talking to her friends.

Ashley thought she would kill him one day.

As was her usual practice, Ashley had retreated to her room after dinner with her family, as soon as she could. Mom and Dad liked to have meals with everyone so that they could converse with each other about their days. To Ashley it was a pain. Not helped by Will telling tales and lying, trying to get her into more trouble.

Her homework done before dinner, Ashley had the television on watching American Idol, dissing the acts with her friends on the computer and the phone, her fingers a whirl as she typed her messages. She was already in her pajamas, zoo animal pants and a plain blue tee shirt.

Ashley's bedroom, her refuge, was quite typical for a girl her age. She wasn't tidy with her stuff so everything was scattered about on the bed and the floor. Her Mom was always telling her off about it and Will would snoop around when she wasn't home. He denied it but she knew he did it.

Ashley's favorite color was purple, so virtually everything in her room was a variation of it, apart from the carpet which was a pale yellow, and the ceiling which was white. When Ashley was forced to clean it up, it was a very pretty room, her bed a mass of pillows and cushions, good quality furniture, flowery drapes that hung to the floor, pictures of seascapes interspersed with her posters of women and men soccer players.

Ashley was spread over her double bed as she typed and watched the acts, and she was relieved when her BFF, or best friend forever, finally texted her after Ashley had sent numerous ones to her, asking what she was doing.

"hey, wer u bin" Ashley asked.

"wth sum cusins they cool cum out & meet em"

"not drssd" Ashley replied.

"only for a sec put coat on"

"ok b rite there"

Ashley's BFF was Sandy, another blonde blue eyed girl, but her hair was shorter, which she was always pushing behind her ears. Not quite as pretty yet as her friend, Sandy had sharper features, especially her cheekbones, that would be an asset to her as an adult. Sandy was also a little taller and even leaner.

Sandy hadn't been aware, but she'd been followed since the previous day upon leaving school with Ashley. When they went their separate ways, Sandy had been trailed to her home, the occupants of the van looking for a suitable spot that was quiet and where they wouldn't be noticed.

Both girls lived in the northern suburbs of Sacramento, in very good neighborhoods where police cars were very rarely seen. Their weekends was a trip to the mall to shop, see a movie, hang out with other friends, and swim at one or the other's backyard pool.

Ashley put on her slippers and went downstairs holding her cellphone, and walked past the family room to the front door. The TV was on loud, so no one heard her say she was just going to the front door step to say hi to Sandy. She slipped on her overcoat that was on the coat stand by the front door.

On opening the door, she was surprised to see Sandy standing beside a large white van on the sidewalk. She was with a woman and a man, in their twenties it looked like to Ashley, and Sandy was still wearing what she wore to school. A short black skirt and a red top beneath her long white cardigan.

"Ash, you need to come and say hello," greeted Sandy, although she sounded a little strange to Ashley.

"I'm not dressed Sandy," replied Ashley in a loud whisper, closing the door behind her, "come to the door."

"It doesn't matter Ash, you look okay, just come and say hi and we'll go."

"Oh okay, but I can't go anywhere or stay out long. I'll get into trouble again."

Ashley made her way over, curious as to why Sandy hadn't changed yet and what her cousins were like. They looked okay. They were smiling as they stood on either side of Sandy, who certainly didn't look her best.

"Are you okay Sandy? You don't look well." Ashley was concerned about her friend as she approached her, holding out her hand.

"I'm sorry Ash," apologized her friend, "they told me they would kill all my family if I didn't get you out here. I'm so sorry." Sandy was crying as she took Ashley's hand in her own, and she was shaking.

"What's going on Sandy?" Asked the now scared Ashley.

"Get in the van girls. Now." Instructed the dark haired man, and he revealed the pistol that he'd been hiding behind Sandy's back. "Now! Get in!"

Ashley hadn't noticed before but the three of them had been standing in front of the open side door of the van. She looked back at her home, praying her Dad was standing at the front door ready to give her hell for going outside in her pajamas. There was no-one there. Nor was there anyone else around. The street was silent and deserted.

"Get in the fucking van," the guy told them through gritted teeth, "Now!"

The woman had lost her smile and she pushed the two girls half into the van, and she told them, "He will shoot you both if you don't get in. Now move."

They stumbled and fell into the van, the man climbing in behind them as the woman slid the door shut and walked calmly to the driver's door, looking around for any signs of anybody, or a drape moving in a window. Nothing. She climbed into the van, started it, and moved slowly and quietly away from the sidewalk and along the street.

In the back of the van, the two girls were huddled together in a corner, while the man was sitting at the back of the van in a chair of some sort. The only light was supplied by a dim wall light attached to a side panel, as the windows were blacked out. At least it was partially comfortable, as the whole rear of the van was padded, but there were straps on the sides and floor.

"Who are these people?" Whispered Ashley.

"I don't know. They grabbed me on my way home from school and said they would shoot Mom, Dad and Kayla if I didn't do what they said. They said they wanted you as well, but when I told them that you were home with your family, we waited somewhere as they listened to the news on the radio. If you hadn't replied to the text they made me send, they would have left you. I'm so sorry Ash, I didn't know what else I could do," sobbed Sandy.

"That's enough chatter," spoke the man approaching them, and he grabbed hold of Sandy and dragged her toward the straps.

"Don't struggle girl, it'll just make it worse for you," he commanded.

Sandy paid him no heed and tried to get away from him, only stopping when he hit her hard in the abdomen with his fist.

"Told you not to do it girl," he said, and directing his voice toward Ashley he continued, "same thing will happen to you if you struggle as well."

He strapped up the wheezing Sandy with both her arms and legs outstretched and then did the same with Ashley.

"Where are you taking us?" Asked Ashley, as she was strapped to the van. "My family don't have much money. They can't afford a ransom."

"We don't want your family's money girl. We just want you and your friend. Now shut up, no more questions, and no more crying."

It was probably another hour before the van stopped and the woman opened the side door.

"Good, they're secure," she said. "Now give them the stuff and you can drive for a while."

They didn't use any names and it was black outside, very quiet.

The woman handed the man a small dark case.

Ashley and Sandy were petrified as they watched the man open the case and they saw the syringes. They both pleaded to be left alone, that they'd promise to be silent and not try to get out of their restraints and run away.

The man ignored them as he took one of the syringes, expelled the air from it, and went to Ashley's left arm. The woman produced a flashlight to give extra light that she shined on Ashley's forearm as the man slapped it.

"Please don't," Ashley pleaded.

He inserted the needle and injected.

After doing the same with the sobbing Sandy, the man and the woman watched as the heroin entered their blood stream.

"First time is always the best," he stated, as the girls calmed down and went into a state of euphoria.

"Go and drive for a while," said the woman, "I'll stay here with them. We'll swop over again when we stop for gas. What did you do with their phones?"

"Dismantled. I'll toss them outside."

The man stepped out of the van without a word and closed the side door on the three females. The woman took her seat at the back and watched the girls, happy faces on them now as the drug took hold, and she checked her gun before relaxing and taking a nap. It was a long drive to their destination.

CHAPTER 3

By the time anyone noticed that Ashley and Sandy were missing, they were not only out of the zip code, they were in a different state.

Frantic calls were made between the two homes and to the police, but no-one had a clue as to where they were.

Sandy had been made to call her Mom when she was snatched, to tell her she was staying over at Ashley's house, which wasn't unusual even on school days. Ashley had also stayed over at Sandy's house many times, so Sandy's Mom wasn't at all worried until Ashley's Mom called, asking if she knew where Ashley was.

Then all hell broke loose.

Police cars were all over the neighborhood and cops were knocking on doors, asking if anyone had seen the two girls or any suspicious people around. No-one had seen a thing.

Ashley's family were beside themselves. They'd been watching TV together and they all knew that Ashley was in her room, watching American Idol. It was only because her TV was still on when her Mom and Dad went to bed, that it caused them to enter her room to turn it off, and realize she wasn't there.

After being questioned by very sympathetic detectives, they determined that Ashley's coat was missing but that she was still wearing her pajamas, and when her Dad checked the house before going to bed, the front door wasn't locked.

Neither Ashley's nor Sandy's phone was available, but after looking at Ashley's computer that was still on, she'd mentioned on her Facebook page that she needed to go outside to say hi to Sandy's cousins that were in town.

Sandy's parents had no idea what that meant as no relatives were visiting, and that Sandy hadn't even come home after school.

The police were worried and called in the FBI, telling the parents that it looked like a possible kidnapping and that was a specialty of the FBI, who would need to tap their phones for possible ransom demands.

Nobody could believe it. How could Ashley just disappear when she's at home, in her bedroom, in her pajamas, and her parents and brothers just yards away.

When the FBI arrived at both houses, setting up their equipment and asking yet more questions, they told the parents that it was probably a kidnapping and that a ransom would no doubt be demanded. When it was, the parents were to demand to speak to their daughters, agreeing to anything, and to stay on the phone for as long as possible to aid the investigation.

What the agents from the FBI did not say, was that they already thought the two girls were the victims of human trafficking, and that within a very short time their lives would be practically ruined. None of the parents had money, two girls being taken together didn't fit the profile of a single pedophile, and it was very rare that pedophiles took two children at the same time or worked in pairs. It was obviously well planned, not a spur of the moment thing.

Ashley and Sandy weren't aware, but they were in the back of the van for nine hours, and they were injected again, this time between the toes, well before they reached their destination.

Their new 'home' was Las Vegas, and it was a very special hotel just off the strip, that catered to guests with certain needs.

The van took the ramp down to the underground parking beneath the forty room hotel, and stopped by the freight elevator. The woman driver had used her card to access the ramp, and she knew she was being watched. She often worked security herself and so knew the system.

On summoning the elevator, two burly men came down with it and they quickly untied Ashley and Sandy. They hustled the two groggy girls into the large elevator and pressed the top floor button, number four. The mousy haired woman and the man from the van were still with them, and when they reached the fourth floor they helped to take them to their rooms.

Like all the other rooms in the hotel, they were very nicely appointed. King beds with pillow top mattresses, en-suite bathrooms with Jacuzzi baths, separate glass showers, flat screen TV's, comfortable sitting areas, and soft carpets. The biggest difference between the girls rooms and those on the floors below, was that there were no phones, no internet hook up, no window latches, no channel changer for the TV, and no door handles. Like all the other rooms, the windows were heavily tinted, so they couldn't be seen from outside even with the lights on, but from these particular windows, you couldn't even see out.

Ashley and Sandy were put into different rooms, but not into or onto their plush beds. They weren't ready for that yet. Instead, they were bundled into small cages with just a rubber mat to lie on. They were very cramped, but in their present state they didn't notice.

None of the four adults had yet to address each other by name. They knew one another, but one of the main rules about working for the hotel was never to address each other by their real names in the presence of any 'guests'.

The two men who had helped situate the two girls were both Mexican, both black haired, adorned with various tattoos, and liked to display their muscles, of which they had plenty.

All the staff in the hotel were required to have a fetish and most of them had convictions for child offenses. Be it young boys, small girls, anal sex, bondage, torture or whatever, anything was accepted. In return, they received their own room in the hotel, free food, a small salary, and time with the 'guests'. It was a very clever ploy, as it created absolute loyalty to the hotel. They weren't prisoners, they could do their own thing away from the hotel, but no visitors were allowed, and as everything in the hotel was recorded for security, they knew that they would be dealt with if they started telling their story. Fatally. Staff did leave, but no one ever talked.

The two Mexicans stayed with the two girls, and the man and the woman returned to the van to meticulously clean it out.

While they were doing that, another man and woman dressed and cleaned up the girls, one at a time, taking pictures of them in staged poses, as they moved them around on their beds. When they were finished, they put them back into the cages.

The abductors, once finished cleaning the van, went to the kitchen and were given a meal and drink. They had a couple of days off now so could relax. They were also given first dibs on the two girls. The woman declined, but wanted a particular young boy further down on the same floor. The man wanted the two girls, even though he was aware he could only do anal sex on them. Their virginity had already been bought for a lot of money by someone else, who was now receiving their photos. It was exactly what he'd ordered.

After the man finished his meal, he made his way to Ashley's room, who was slowly coming out of her drugged haze. It was important that she was aware of what her future entailed.

Opening the door of her cage, he went right at it. Removing the new pajama bottoms that had been put on her after the photo session, he ignored her protests and screams, and as he was much stronger than Ashley, she couldn't fight him off. He loved her trying to fight, it was heaven to him.

Dropping his pants to his knees, he prepared her by using his fingers, and when she started crying he smiled as he inserted his penis into her anus. For Ashley it was terrifying, painful, and humiliating. She didn't want to be an adult any more, she just wanted to go home to her family as she sobbed, feeling his hands groping her as he pumped into her, and then the warm liquid as he came.

She was still sobbing as he left and she thought her world had ended, but it just got worse. No sooner had the man from the van left than the other two men came back. Encouraging each other, they also fucked her in the ass, one after the other. It was grotesque, and she wanted another injection.

Sandy went through the same thing, but her ordeal lasted longer as the three men needed more time to come.

Over the next few days, both girls were continually abused by both men and one woman, taught what to do to men and women to please them, and injected with more of the drug that they were now dependent on. They were also introduced to ecstasy. Ashley and Sandy didn't see each other. They were taken to the bathroom and watched while they used the toilet and took a shower, and lost track of the days and the date. Neither had any inkling of how long they had been there. All the time they were told not to resist or their families would be killed, and they described in gruesome detail the fate that would befall them if they didn't behave.

For the whole time, they were kept in their cages. Food and drink was brought to them, as was fresh clothing. Most of the time they felt numb and in a horrible nightmare.

When their cages were finally removed, they had no idea what was going on, but the beds felt nice to both of them.

Sandy was picked first, and even in her drugged state she wasn't happy with the fat man in his sixties who entered her room before she'd even had chance to sleep on her new king size bed. The man was gross and smelled of stale sweat and aftershave.

He instructed her to call him 'Daddy', which she did but felt disgusted by it. When he entered her vagina she screamed with the pain, which made him laugh, and he kissed her with his smelly mouth. Sandy was exactly what he'd paid for. A blonde minor who was a virgin who he could screw in a controlled setting, and knew how to please him.

He took Ashley the following day, and she was as sickened as her best friend, as the old man came into her and slobbered all over her.

No sooner had the girls showered, cried and crawled into their beds, than someone else was entering their room and putting their hands and then their penises between their legs and forcing their way inside. It seemed never ending, and all both girls wanted was more of the drugs and to just go home.

CHAPTER 4

Bec was a 10 year old girl in the Philippines that her parents couldn't afford to feed anymore. When a stranger offered them enough money to feed the rest of their family for the next two years, they had to take the money. So they sold their daughter.

Along with many others in her very poor neighborhood, Bec was transported by ship to America. She had no idea where she was going, nor did any of the others she was with, and they all struggled with sea sickness as they comforted each other in the hold of the huge container ship.

After what seemed like weeks, they were put in a container with just a few tiny holes for air, and they felt themselves being lifted then dropped, and there they remained, with no water, food, or toilet. It got very rancid, hot, and overpowering.

Just as Bec thought she was going to die in the metal box, the door finally opened and she and the other children practically fell and rushed into the fresh open air. Three of them didn't, they'd fainted, and they were dragged out.

None of the children were aware of it, but they were now in New Jersey and it was cold and dark. They huddled together to try to stay warm, as they were watched over by unsmiling men with guns and rifles. They were all scared witless and whenever anyone spoke, one of the men would tell them to shush, making the sound while holding a finger to their mouth.

When a tractor trailer pulled up they all groaned as they were herded into it, but at least this one smelt clean for now. Finding a small space to sit down on, Bec buried her head in her hands as others sobbed and wailed.

At least they weren't in the trailer long this time. Very soon, they came to a halt and they were all forced out. The same men as before, along with a couple more and two women, arranged them all into a line and they escorted them into the huge building from the deserted car lot.

Once inside, it seemed like a maze of corridors to Bec as they walked along the concrete floors, and then they were in a large changing room with benches lining the walls, that had individual spaces for clothing and belongings.

One of the women was Filipino, and she instructed all the children to take off all of their filthy clothing and leave them on the floor. As they all undressed, she bawled out the ones who tried to keep their underwear on, threatening them with a beating if they didn't comply.

Once they were all naked, the woman told them to go into the next room and take a shower, making sure to use the soap that was provided.

Bec had felt dirty for quite some time. She, like all the others, was still in the same clothing that she'd been taken in, so was glad to hear that she could now wash herself. To find that the long row of showers was also hot was even better. Nobody was allowed to take excessive time showering, as there weren't enough spaces for everybody, and as soon as someone stepped out, then another took their place.

Bec was very pretty, small and slim. Her long black hair was very straight and half way down her back. Her oval shaped face contained brown eyes that had natural long lashes, a small nose, and perfect teeth behind her pink lips. The bangs that hung down to her eyebrows only enhanced her cuteness.

No-one was aware of it, but Bec could also get by in English. Her family had needed her to go begging on a daily basis and so she had picked up a lot of the language from the tourists. Being street wise even at her young age, she didn't want anyone to know she could understand anything said in English.

When everyone had showered, the kids were handed towels and as they dried themselves, the Filipino woman yelled that they were to return to the changing room and to sit down on the benches.

Doing as they were told, and trying to conceal their modesty with the towels, they sat around the room wondering what was going to happen to them next. With the men in the corners of the room brandishing their guns, the Filipino woman addressed them all from the center of the room.

Bec thought the woman was around fifty years old. Although she was small, she looked tough and her features were rough and unsmiling. Wearing a black trouser suit and her black hair in a bun, she told them in their native language that they would be given new clothes, they would be pictured, and that they would spend the night in a special place before they were taken to their new homes.

She went on to say that their parents had sold them, that they now belonged to other people, who would keep them until they had worked off the debt that was owed. It had cost a lot of money to buy them and to transport them to another country, and it was costing a lot more money to clothe them, feed them, and to keep them safe. Their new owners would treat them well and take care of them until they'd gotten their money's worth, but after that they would be given documents, and they would be free to do as they wished here in America. However, if anyone tried to run away or didn't do as they were told, then they would be severely punished, perhaps killed, and their parents would have to pay back the money they'd be given. If they didn't, then they would be killed and their other children would be taken away. Also, from this day on, everyone was to forget their names as they would be given new ones by their new owners.

None of the children doubted that she was telling the truth. She instilled fear in all of them.

Trolleys were pushed around the room and the children were given underwear, plain white gym shoes, polo shirts, and elastic waisted pants. The women made sure everyone's hair was neat by using combs or brushes, and then they were all ushered into another room.

Bec knew what this room was. It was a basketball court and it was surrounded by hundreds of seats. It was huge.

A camera had been set up at one side of the court and it faced a white sheet. Each child was given a number that was on a card and hung over their necks, with the same number put on their shirt with a sharpie.

All the children were made to smile at the camera. Some had to have their tears wiped away, and several photos were taken of each kid.

Once all the photos were taken, the children were taken out of the building and put in the trailer again, wondering what was going to happen next.

They weren't in it for long, and soon they were being shepherded into some kind of warehouse that had cots set up for them, but just one bathroom between them all. Bec thought that because of there being no shower facilities, they had to be taken somewhere else to wash themselves.

Bec had figured that there were about a hundred kids in all, maybe more, now homeless and in a foreign country with no family or friends. She was as scared as everyone else.

Sandwiches had been provided as well as water for everyone, and all the kids tucked into them after being instructed to throw the plastic wrapping and the empty bottles into the two large refuse bins. Once they'd eaten and drank, they were to go to their cots and sleep. All the cots were numbered, so they also had to make sure they were in the right one.

Bec's cot was between the two children who had been beside her in the basketball arena, so there was now a little familiarity between them. One was a boy about her age, and a girl on the other side who looked a few years older.

Before she was told to be quiet, the older girl whispered to Bec to write down her full name and home address whenever she got the opportunity to, and to keep it somewhere safe. She also told Bec to tell the boy to do the same, just in case something happened to them. She also said to do exactly what she was told, not to answer back, and to watch and listen.

Bec and the boy were now shaking with fear, even being on the streets begging felt safer than being in this warehouse.

Thankfully, they were so tired they eventually fell asleep.

CHAPTER 5

While the children were sleeping, their photos had been posted online and each child was being auctioned off to the highest bidder. No matter who it was.

For the sellers, it was the most dangerous part of the operation as the FBI were known to monitor websites for human trafficking, and if caught, you spent years in jail.

It was like smuggling drugs. High risk of being caught, but huge rewards if you weren't. Everyone was aware of it, and they knew that if they were caught then they couldn't talk, or there would be serious consequences to either themselves or to the people they loved. They were constantly reminded of this with news clippings of people who had co-operated with the FBI, or ICE, to reduce their sentences, and then of the repercussions of doing so. Human trafficking is a very serious business, with billions of dollars generated throughout the world. Important and influential people were not only behind the trafficking, but also customers too, so if a few people died along the way then so be it. Traffickers as well as victims.

Most of the customers were regulars, so they could let them know about the new secure website that had been created for these events, giving them a code to enter, and they would have their financial details on a secure record.

Anyone new had to be endorsed by an existing customer, checked again, then their financial details were taken. No-one was given credit, all the kids had to be paid for up front, and once done then they would be delivered to them at a remote location.

The auction was still going on as the children were waking up and lining up to use the bathroom. More food had been provided. Doughnuts and cream cheese bagels, along with bottles of water. Again the kids were instructed to dispose of the plastic wrapping and empty bottles in the trash cans.

The children had no idea about the auction. They were doing that from a different location, so they were told to wait by their cots and not to talk.

The auction itself had started with the older kids, as they wouldn't get as much for them, and finished with the very youngest.

It had been a few weeks since a batch like this had arrived in the New York area, so there was a lot of interest. Physical details had been added to the photos to generate more interest. Usually, the children would be dressed provocatively, with make up on the girls, but as there were so many this time, they'd kept to the polo shirt uniform. Most of the customers wanted to know if the kids were virgins, had pubic hair yet, if the girls breasts had formed at all, if puberty had been reached, or if the boys had been circumcised. Some wanted chubby kids, others slim or athletic. There were no white kids in this batch, they were the big bucks, but the Asians were very popular as they always did as they were told and didn't need as many drugs.

Within a short time of the auction starting, thousands of dollars were being deposited, arrangements were being made, and once they'd eaten, the kids started to get moved to their destinations.

Some went in groups, others singly or with one or two others. It was all down to the buyers.

Bec went alone. She was put into the back of a small box van with its windows blacked out, and she estimated that she was in there for about an hour, before the driver stopped and came around to open the door.

Getting out into the warm day, Bec was met by a woman who handed over her driver's license to the van driver, who handed it back after checking her name and looking at her face. The driver then got back into his van and drove away.

They were in a rest area in the midst of many trees and no one else was around. For all Bec knew, she could be killed here by this woman and left to rot.

The woman herself was dark haired and attractive, slim, and wearing a pink sweater over her black jeans. Her hands were covered in various rings, and earrings dangled from her ears below her shoulder length wavy hair. She was around 5' 9'' in her heels, sharp features, highlighted by copious make up. She spoke bossily, like a schoolteacher, and held a gun.

"English?" She asked.

Bec shook her head no.

"I suppose you have no luggage and no clothes. Okay, so be it, we need to go," the woman continued, "before we get seen."

She signaled to Bec to go to her vehicle, an SUV, and opened the rear passenger door for her to get in. She then indicated to Bec to lie down by putting her head sideways on to her hands, so Bec complied. Once she was lying down, the woman reached over the back of the seat and retrieved a blanket, covering Bec from head to toe. She then closed the door on her and went to the driver's door, opening it and then getting in, starting the engine before closing the door. She then drove without speaking for almost another hour. Bec stayed still.

When the car stopped, Bec heard a door opening, they then moved slowly forward a few yards before the engine was turned off, and Bec heard the door again. The woman got out of the car, and after opening the door to Bec, took off the blanket and Bec could see they were in a garage.

The woman motioned to her to get out, and after walking through the connecting door into the house, she opened another door that led down into the basement. Putting the light on, she escorted Bec down the stairs and Bec found that the large room contained not only a washer and dryer, but also a table to fold clothes on, a furnace and water heater, an iron and a board. It also contained a very large bed and armchair, along with a bathroom.

The woman pointed to the bed and then to Bec, and also pointed to the bathroom. She then left Bec there as she went back upstairs and locked the door behind her.

Bec took a look around, also finding a fridge and a microwave, and clothing in a closet. Clothing that would fit her. The bathroom was large, had toothpaste and a new brush, soaps, shampoos, hair brush, cotton balls, towels, everything. Except anything sharp.

On looking through the nightstands, Bec found some things she didn't recognize, but also some magazines with adults having sex with children. Then she cried as she fell backwards onto the king sized bed.

CHAPTER 6

Ashley's parents were still in shock many weeks later. No ransom demand had ever materialized, the FBI had gone, and no one had any idea or clue as to where their daughter had gone. They couldn't get over the fact that one minute she had been safe in her bedroom, the next she had disappeared, like she had never existed.

Ashley's younger brother Will and the older Greg couldn't understand it either. Despite their differences, they loved their sister and wanted her back, neither thinking she'd just run away with her best friend. Not Ashley. If she'd run away it would have been with her phone, laptop, money and clothing. Although her phone was missing, it was turned off, and Ashley never turned off her phone. It was always glued to her ear.

Since that awful night when they realized she was missing, and the police and the FBI had swarmed over the house and the neighborhood, they had posted pictures of Ashley and Sandy on every available space. When the posters had faded or been torn, they replaced them, and kept asking total strangers if they had seen either of them.

Both sets of the missing girls parents had fallen out, blaming each other's daughter for their own loss, in a futile attempt of making sense of it all.

Will and Greg stayed out of that argument. They both knew Sandy and didn't attach any blame on her, thinking she must have been forced to entice Ashley out of the house.

The FBI had mentioned eventually that they thought both girls had been taken by Human Traffickers. It fitted their profile and if so, then the girls could now be anywhere. But alive. If anyone else had taken them, then the chances were that the girls were already deceased. They knew that Sandy must have been kept somewhere before Ashley was picked up, but there had been no leads on that. The only other explanation was that they had run away, but as there had been no threat of doing so, or of taking anything with them, the chances of that were extremely slim.

Every day, Will or Greg would go into the police station and ask if they had discovered something new about Ashley and Sandy. The shake of the head with a sad face told them no, but they persevered, not wanting to give up on their sister, who after all, was probably still alive somewhere, waiting for help, wanting to come home.

The human trafficking aspect shocked both families. The slave trade had been abolished one hundred and fifty years ago, and now the FBI were saying they were slaves. Here? In the USA? That couldn't be right.

The FBI didn't want to alarm the families, but when it became clear that the girls hadn't been kidnapped for a ransom, and neither family had much money to spare, they had to tell them that the girls were either dead, or enduring a living hell. People paid a lot of money for cute twelve year old girls, especially Caucasian with blonde hair. Hopefully, they would get to them before too long, help them recover, and return them home.

Once told this, the families searched the web, horrified by stories told by freed or escaped victims, who were drugged and repeatedly raped, forgetting who they were or where they were from, bodies ruined, and riddled with disease.

Whenever Will and Greg felt like just giving up, they reminded each other of what was probably happening to Ashley. They would go and post more pictures, and update her status on the Facebook page they'd created for her and Sandy, and also the website.

Sometimes, someone would leave a comment saying that a person had been arrested in their town or state for imprisoning a minor, and they would enquire about it, usually at the police station, but with no luck. Most comments were to encourage them in their search, and not to give up on the two girls.

CHAPTER 7

Ashley and Sandy were already addicted to their drugs. Their captors didn't want them to have needle marks all over their arms so they made sure they injected them through the feet. Customers didn't want kids with blemished skin.

Nobody ever referred to them by their real names, and the drugs were making them lose all sense of who they were, what day or time it was, or even how old they were. Even after such a short time, they were just following orders, doing whatever the captors or the customers wanted. No matter what it was.

They had women customers as well as men, which they both generally preferred as most of the women were gentler unless they liked to use the 'toys' on them. Whatever happened, Ashley and Sandy had to give pleasure, otherwise they would be given more rougher customers, and more often. So they did. They'd learned from the captors how to fake orgasms, what to do with their bodies to convince the customers, and how to make the men come quicker. They got good at it and were getting popular. But all the while, they were threatened with violence and no drugs if they didn't do as they were told.

Between customers, and while the girls took the required shower, housekeepers entered their rooms to change the sheet they'd had sex on. The customers normally wanted them to be fully visible, so the girls usually pulled back the duvets. If the customer wanted sex on the floor or on the chair, and didn't use a condom, the housekeeper would wipe away the stain. The housekeeper would also check the pillows for stains and smells, change the pillowcases if needed, then spray the room with air freshener before leaving.

Very soon, Ashley and Sandy were allowed to vacate their rooms when they had a break, and go to the sitting room/kitchen. They were still monitored in there, were allowed to chat, but not permitted to use their real names or talk about where they thought they were.

While they were in there, it gave the housekeepers chance to clean their rooms and bathrooms properly, and stock up the soaps, toothpastes, body washes, tampons, condoms and pads.

Ashley and Sandy's only clothes now were negligees, erotic underwear, bras that they didn't yet need, teddies, and school uniforms that were tight and very short. Other than that, all they had were pajamas which they slept in and wore to the sitting room.

There was no regular TV in the sitting room, or in their rooms, but they could watch a movie or one of the soap operas that was recorded by the captors. In their bedroom it was continuous porn. There was also a radio that had no news stations on it, just music, books and magazines.

The adjoining kitchen was always staffed, meals were cooked for them, but no access was given to the stove or to the knives.

Getting into the large sitting room with its comfortable armchairs and couches, meant you could see and meet others who were in the same predicament. Ashley, even in her haze, could tell some were younger than her and a few older. Boys as well as girls, different races and colors.

Ashley and Sandy had met kids from Mexico, Cambodia, Thailand and Japan. Most had picked up a little English but not much, mainly what they'd heard in their bedrooms and from the captors.

One or two they'd met did speak English, and they told Ashley and Sandy out of earshot of their captors, that some of them had been tortured for not doing what they were told, with skewers and cattle prods inserted into them, or strangled until they passed out. It was emphasized to them to behave and do as they were told, or they would suffer in the same horrible ways.

The older ones were worried about being cast out. Whenever newcomers arrived, space had to be made for them and it was nearly always one of the elders who was taken away. They didn't know where, they thought it was either to be killed and buried somewhere, or just dumped on a strange street with no money and nowhere to go. They were so scared of being selected to leave.

Someone had heard from an overheard conversation that a new batch had arrived, and they were being kept in their rooms at the moment while they were being taught the ropes. It was always an exciting time for the staff as they could enjoy the newbies before the customers.

This made life very uncomfortable for the older ones, as they knew they would shortly be surplus to requirements.

The decision was made elsewhere within a matter of days. The oldest six, whose value had steadily decreased in the passing years, would make way for the new batch, who would command much greater fees. The fees that had been paid for them would be recovered their first day of work, if not trebled.

A decision was also made on the fate of the soon to be departed, and all the staff were asked for their opinions. It was an important question and all the staff took it seriously. Most of them were already in parole violation for moving away from their home states and not telling anyone, or reporting to the local police. It was hard for sex offenders to lead a free life after being released, and this was as close as it got for some of them. They all knew that one tip to the police would send them all back to prison, so they were extremely careful with their views.

The final outcome was that two of the six were taken to the desert, and after pleading for their lives and offering sexual favors, they were shot and buried. The favors were taken, but they were still killed.

The other four, all women, were sold to a pimp in Reno, with just the clothes they were in and heavily drugged. Two of them wandered away during the first night, confused and disoriented. When they awoke in a dirty alley, they had no idea where they were, where they'd been, or who they were. All they knew was that they needed some 'smack'.

When they were at the hotel, although they'd be given regular dosages of drugs, they had also been forced to eat. Customers didn't want skeletons so everyone had to eat. On the streets, the addicts spend nearly all of their money when they got any, on drugs. The two women though weren't on the streets long. They were picked up by the police as they stood on a street corner, and it was obvious to the police that they were new to the area, as they were soliciting different streets from all the other hookers. They had no ID's and no records. They didn't know who they were. Nor did they have an address to go home to, or any clothing or belongings.

CHAPTER 8

Bec had been brought some food in her basement room, then was left there alone for almost another hour. She was still trembling.

Bec wondered what her parents had been told when they sold her, and if they imagined their little girl being here. Bec had taken the threats against her family seriously. She had no doubt they would all be killed if she didn't do as she was told, so she was stuck.

When the door opened at the top of the stairs, she huddled herself tightly, as the two adults made their way down the wooden steps.

The same woman as before led the way. She looked differently now, out of her day wear. She was wearing a sheer short nightdress in white, a white g string, and a red lipped smile.

The man with her was just in boxers. He was as fit as the woman, black hair neatly combed back, and prominent chest hair.

Dressed, they would look like an attractive executive couple.

The woman sat down on the bed next to Bec and put her arm around her shoulders, and with her other hand she wiped the tears away from Bec's cheeks.

Lifting Bec's head, she pointed to herself with the hand she'd used to wipe tears and said, "Me, Ma'am," then pointed to the man and said "Sir". She repeated it a couple of times to Bec. Then pointing at Bec, she said "Baby"

The woman undressed Bec as they sat on the edge of the bed, then stood to undress herself, the man watching intently. She took out one of the magazines and rifled through the pages until she found what she was looking for, sat back down next to Bec, and pointed at the picture.

Bec looked and gathered her nerve, then stroked the woman as the pictures showed. It seemed to please the woman and she lay back, taking Bec's hand and showing her how to use it. After a while, with the woman softly moaning, she released Bec's hand and grasped the back of her head, bringing her lips to her own. She forced her tongue into Bec's mouth, and pulled her body on top of herself, her hands stroking the small body. She then guided Bec downwards, over her breasts and down to between her legs, making more moaning noises as she did so.

As the man made motions to move behind Bec, the woman stopped him and turned Bec over, going down on her. As she did so, the man straddled Bec and put a cushion under her head, as he moved his erect penis toward her mouth.

Bec had seen the pictures and knew what she had to do and almost threw up as she did so.

When the woman stopped licking her, she tapped the man on his shoulder who removed his penis from Bec's mouth and put it between her legs. Bec screamed as he forced his way into her, a broad smile on the man's face as he began to pump, and the woman watched encouraging him.

For Bec it seemed like hours before a warm liquid entered her and he slowly withdrew himself, kissing the woman very passionately.

Bec watched and desperately wanted to go and bathe herself, but the woman, after putting her g string back on and her nightie, signaled to Bec to follow, handing her the tray that Bec had eaten from.

Bec put on a long tee shirt before following the two adults up the steps, and they took her to the kitchen sink which was full of dirty dishes. The woman signaled to her to do the dishes, and showed her where the soap and sponge were, along with the dishwasher, towels, and where the various things went.

As Bec went about it, the man began playing with the woman, and very soon they were having sex as they both watched her wash dishes, her presence seeming to excite them both.

After Bec finished, she waited uncomfortably as they finally climaxed, and then the woman took her back downstairs. She pointed to a clock and made 'beep beep' noises, then pointed upstairs.

Once she'd left, Bec took her shower, scrubbing herself before falling asleep, only being awoken by the alarm clock.

When she went upstairs after hearing the door being unlocked, the woman was waiting for her and took her around the house. She indicated and silently mouthed words for what she wanted Bec to do.

Vacuum, dust, make the bed, pick up laundry, do dishes, sweep, wipe down, clean the bathroom.

Bec knew what the woman wanted, and went about it. Every day. At night and at weekends the couple would play with her intimately, either alone or with each other, and Bec wondered if the other children had it as bad as she did.

The woman had a nasty streak about her. The things that Bec had found in the nightstand and didn't know what they were, the woman did. She especially liked to use them when she was alone with Bec, to hurt her, which she enjoyed doing.

The woman was also prone to punishing Bec with slaps if she didn't think she was doing a good enough job around the house, and yelling at her.

Bec still pretended not to talk or understand English, and she thought that made her life a little easier.

Bec wasn't allowed out front, or to go anywhere, but she could go in the back yard that was surrounded by a wooden eight foot fence. She had to cut the grass out there once a week. She had learned from the mail that was left around, that the two people she was with were called Jane and Robert McGrady, and they lived in somewhere called New Jersey. She had no idea where New Jersey was, had never heard of it, but she made a note of it along with her real name and address which she kept very hidden.

Apart from the grass in the back yard, there was little else apart from a barbecue, some plastic chairs, and a small dogwood tree at the back of the yard. If ma'am got really mad, like when she came home and found her husband unexpectedly at home screwing Bec, she would tie Bec to the tree and leave her out there, no matter what the weather. It was okay if it was sunny, but when it was cold and wet, Bec would shelter as best she could and hug the tree for a little warmth.

Although Bec was no longer locked in or had a gun pointed in her direction, she was still terrified of what would happen to her family if she ran away. Besides, there was no place to run to.

CHAPTER 9

In a large Washington house, very close to Embassy Row, the specialty was boys and young men. The owners of the house were Justin and Troy Reynolds, who had been legally married in the state of New York and ran an art gallery. Although they were betrothed, they had always had an open relationship and looked forward to hearing about each other's exploits.

Before they met and went into business together, Troy had often frequented various homes where he'd been able to enjoy young boys. Before then, he'd frequented public restrooms for rent boys, which was highly dangerous, or gay bars, for an evening partner.

He much preferred the younger boys with their smooth skins and slender frames, but it was difficult to acquire them without being arrested. So when he was put forward as a customer to one of the trafficker houses, he leapt at it. It didn't feel seedy, he wasn't looked at like a pervert, and he didn't need to keep looking over his back. He became a regular. That he was raping a boy never entered his head.

At that time he was an interior designer, and he looked and filled the part. You only had to look at him or hear him speak to guess he was possibly gay, but he was very popular and made a good living.

He met Justin whilst attending an art exhibition, and although Justin was a fully grown adult, he looked young and he kept his skin shaved and very smooth. Like himself, Justin was slim and fairly tall, favored tight clothing, used a lot of hand expressions, and was very polite. They could even wear each other's wardrobes, so close were they in size. The biggest difference between them was that Justin was blonde to Troy's dark brown, which was all curls compared to Justin's straightness.

Right from the word go, the two men saw others as they got to know one another, and had no problem with it. When Troy confessed to Justin that he sometimes had sex with young boys, Justin was jealous and wanted to do the same. Troy introduced Justin to the house he frequented.

They moved in together into Troy's apartment and carried on with their occupations, until one day, whilst chatting, wondered about keeping their own boys, and how they would do it.

After a couple of bottles of wine, they both agreed that having their own art gallery house would be perfect, and that each of them would be able to find many customers.

So they took the plunge, getting heavily into debt with buying the large house, and making the alterations. They thought they would never see the end of the huge debts they'd accrued.

Until they got some boys in after paying yet more money they didn't have.

The advice they'd received about buying virgin boys really paid off. The amounts of money that folk would pay for being the first to penetrate the boys was ridiculous and amazing. They were easily able to get out of debt, and were now flourishing.

They never needed to advertise. They had all the contacts they needed and they ranged from law enforcement, to very high end folk on Capitol Hill. To an observer, the visitors to the art gallery home all seemed in need of paintings and objects d'art and Troy and Justin were happy to oblige them.

It was a perfect way to mask the business, and if anyone asked questions, the art was real. It just wasn't worth as much as they'd paid for it.

As owners went, Troy and Justin were unusual in that they cared in some way. They looked after their boys with regular medical checks with one of the customers, made them comfortable, and once they had repaid their debt to Troy and Justin, they could go. Of course, the debt was paid off almost instantly, but Troy and Justin would allow them to leave eventually, or even stay on, as a couple of young men had.

The house itself was four levels with a basement. The top floor was exclusive to the boys, but it was all self-sufficient with a kitchen, bathrooms, laundry, sitting area. They could also take the small elevator down to the basement where there was a pool, games room, Jacuzzi, wet bar, bathroom, and large screen TV.

The only ones who were allowed to leave the house were the older boys, who now worked and earned money from Troy and Justin, but they were not allowed visitors. They did the cooking, the cleaning with help from the boys, and the shopping.

Due to their location, no notice was ever taken of the visitors that frequented the house. Nobody ever saw the young boys either. It was just two gay guys who liked to party and sell their art, and the influential people said it was all good harmless fun. So they were left alone.

Unless arrangements had been pre-ordered, such as a new boy with no experience, then the customers would just go to the house, make a selection from the parade of who was there, then go to a room. It was very sociable with drinks and snacks, very calm and extremely relaxed.

Justin and Troy always did the training of the boys. They'd learned from bitter experience that they couldn't just throw the boys at the first high paying customer. They needed to learn things first, and Troy and Justin enjoyed doing it, trying to be gentle, even when the boys cried as they always did. They always thought the boys were much more enjoyable than after they had been with a few customers, so they relished the early days when they were naive and innocent. It wasn't rape in Justin's and Troy's view, it was teaching.

They had recently purchased two boys. One that had been in the cot next to Bec, and a slightly older one who was just a tad taller, with longer hair. Both boys shared the same brown skin and brown eyes, they were very slender, had good even teeth, and were very handsome.

Justin and Troy didn't like to torture their boys, but they did use heroin to begin with. They didn't keep administering it as others did, but for the first weeks or so they did. The older boys would wean them off it, and administer punishment if they tried to escape. The boys were constantly reminded they were in a foreign country, their family's didn't want them back, and they had no money or papers. If they ran away, they would end up in a far worse place and would probably be killed. However, if they stayed, they would be looked after and would eventually be able to leave if they wished to. All they had to do was obey the instructions, and soon they would actually enjoy it.

The younger boy, even in his drugged state, wanted to bite off Troy's penis when he was forced to take it into his mouth, and almost gagged with the smell and feel of it. He didn't know which was worse, the oral or the anus, he just hated it all.

He resolved to himself to just do as he was told, not to think about it, and remember who he was. Justin and Troy didn't use his real name, and no one else was allowed to either, and by the time they thought he was ready for a customer, he was going by the name of Matthew.

The other boy took a little longer before he was declared ready. Although he did everything asked of him, he couldn't stop crying. Even with extra heroin, he would constantly cry or sob when alone in a room with Troy or Justin, and then a week after 'Matthew' had been put with his first customer, he just seemed to give up. Whatever sparkle left in his eyes disappeared, he became numb to it all.

'Matthew's' first customer was extremely well dressed and was in his fifties. His black hair was being overtaken by grey, his suit masked his out of shape body, and his breath smelled of cigars.

'Matthew's' uniform was a flowery dress shirt, tight black pants, and flip flops. All the other clothing that he had to wear was very similar, and he hated it. He just didn't say so.

No chatting about general things was allowed by either party, so 'Matthew' couldn't ask, in his very limited English, what his customer did for a living, where he lived, or anything else personal. He was instructed instead to praise the customer and to moan in delight at whatever was being done to him.

That first customer though made 'Matthew' bleed. At first he thought the man had come heavily, but the blood kept oozing well after the man had finished, and it had hurt. He'd been much more forceful than either Troy or Justin, and they weren't too pleased when they were summoned upstairs by one of the older boys to inspect the damage.

Not that they did anything. The customer had paid extremely well to take 'Matthew's' virginity, or so he thought. They just told the older boy to take Matthew into the shower and make him wait there until the blood stopped running. Once it did, he could be sent back downstairs for another customer who was patiently waiting.

The other boy was now known as 'Gerald', and when he eventually got his first customer, he went through the ordeal with no emotion whatsoever. He was well and truly broken.

'Matthew' could see this even at his own tender age, 'Gerald' was living in his own little world and just doing whatever he was told without any comment or idle chatter. 'Matthew' vowed to himself not to give in, no matter how long it would take to get away from this hell.

CHAPTER 10

In Plano, Texas, a city just north of Dallas, lived a man named Richard Brand. He was a bitter man, forever tainted with the stigma of being a sexual offender. Even after serving his time in prison where he was grouped with other child molesters and rapists, he still had it hanging over him with constant visits from the parole officer and the police. It was a nightmare.

Richard had once been a youthful teacher, and a young girl, Kimberley, had come into his empty classroom one day after school, and had taken her clothes off. What could he do? It wasn't his fault. Kimberley was beautiful, wanted him to fuck her, so he obliged her. Nothing wrong with that. Biggest problem was that Kimberley was only fourteen and he got caught with his pants down. Literally. He'd been paying for it ever since, with his freedom and career gone and the police always questioning him and looking at him like an alien.

Richard's mother had died while he was in prison, no doubt with the shame of her only son being the cause of her fatal heart attack. Richard's father had left when Richard was arrested, and he'd never heard from him again.

At least Richard had a home, his family home that he'd inherited on his Mother's death. There was no work for him anymore. Nobody would hire a convicted sex offender, so he lived on social security.

Since being released, Richard had been working on his house, being careful about where he bought materials, but most often stealing them from building sites.

Richard's father had been a builder so he'd often helped him with things, and when he departed it was with such haste, that he'd left all of his tools and books. It was perfect for Richard's plan.

Not only was Richard checked on regularly, but also all of his internet surfing was looked at as well. Every time someone came, they wanted to look at the computer, and they were always asking why he had looked at the sites he'd gone to. Was it unusual for someone to go to amazon.com?

Working on the house had been hard toil for Richard, but it had helped remove the weight he'd gained in prison, although the parole officer thought he was slow in what he was doing. The parole officer just wasn't seeing the real work he'd been doing.

Richard had begun by very carefully cutting out the fitted carpet in his old bedroom closet and the wooden floor beneath it. He had then re-attached the carpet to the wood and then put the whole thing back, but this time with invisible hinges so that the whole thing lifted up from the side with a hidden latch. He also packed the underneath of what was now a door, with insulation and plywood, so that it wouldn't sound hollow if knocked on.

Once he was satisfied with that, he began the arduous work of digging beneath it.

As he dug, he made wooden braces and poured concrete to make everything stable, and the earth he removed was disposed of around the back yard, which he was re-landscaping and also building a garden shed. He was able to put a lot of the earth behind the back yard fence, which was waste land that led down to a creek, with many trees to shield him as he did so.

The house itself was ranch style with just one level. All his neighbors knew he was a sex offender, and whenever he went out and happened to see one, they would turn their back to him. If he happened to be in the front yard, folk would cross the street rather than walk past him, and kids would call him a pervert if they were out of earshot of their parents.

Richard hadn't changed much inside the house. He had taken over the master bedroom and made it a little more masculine, but not very much as he didn't have the money to spend on it. His mother had kept up with certain things like TV's, her furnishings were comfortable, and he felt close to her being back in her house. A lot of her clothing still remained in the closets and drawers, and Richard was slowly sorting them out and taking them to the Salvation Army. Much of his father's stuff still remained along with the tools, but most of it was useless to Richard, although he did keep some of the clothing to work in.

The house was like most of the others in the neighborhood in that it fitted in, and it was one of the better kept homes on the street. It also felt warm and inviting to the select people who entered it, watched closely by neighbors behind their drapes.

Richard was balding now and he had to wear glasses. His looks that had attracted the young Kimberley were a distant memory now, and when he looked through his Mom's photo albums he barely recognized himself.

When he was arrested, Richard was single but was seeing a couple of women, living alone in his rented apartment, and he met up with his buddies on weekends to drink beer and watch sports. He felt he was a normal guy, and he never envisaged being seduced by a child. His bitterness made him dig harder. He'd show them. At least this time he'd be able to savor the child. The one thing he'd never told anyone, was that he really enjoyed Kimberley, and would have had sex with her again and again if they hadn't been caught. This time, no one would catch him.

He cut, sawed, hammered, dug, braced, and hauled the rubble, careful all the time in case there was a surprise visitor. The building sites were a treasure trove, and what he took would be barely noticed. A few pipes, some wires, a sink, a shower basin and head, pumps, a toilet, microwave, shelving, wooden supports, and lots of insulation.

The final touch was dismantling his old bed and then reassembling it in his new cellar, and also hooking up a TV which he turned on to full volume to check for noise. He couldn't hear it above, nor outside, even by the hidden air vent. It was perfect.

He thought if he could just avoid being seen by anyone, he'd be home safe.

Waiting until it was dusk, Richard drove his mother's now old suburban toward Dallas, stopping at the high end shops in the Highland Park area. A lot of rich families lived in that part of town, and their kids felt safe with an attitude that only came from being wealthy.

Richard didn't want to loiter around or be suspicious in any way, he just wanted a particular kind of girl to break away so that he could pick her up.

He had a couple of false alarms, but the first girl wasn't right, and the second was picked up by her parents within seconds. Looking at his watch, he knew the window would be closing soon, so was delighted when he spotted a girl bidding her friends goodnight with hugs, before she set off alone, presumably to her nearby home.

Richard had to drive around the block out of sight of her and thought she'd be long gone, but he caught sight of her heading up a street by the local golf course. He headed for the street, turned, and saw her. There were no houses on either side of her, but many further ahead once she passed the course.

He drove ahead of her, his heart beating crazily as he summoned up the nerve to do this. The girl was just right. Very slim, long black hair, and blossoming into a young woman.

Stopping before coming to any houses, which were like mansions to Richard's eyes, he slammed the driver's door as he got out, kicking the rear tires as he made his way around the vehicle and opening the rear passenger door. He was cursing as the girl approached, and being a polite Texan girl she enquired if everything was okay.

Getting his first good look at her, Richard thought he was in love, her blue eyes dazzled him as he clenched his fist and hit her hard on the chin.

He grabbed her as she collapsed, and threw her onto the back seat of the Suburban, closing the door behind her and casually walking around to the driver's door. He wanted to get out of there as fast as he could, and he had to fight the panic, looking around to see if there were any witnesses or lights coming on from the nearby houses. Nothing. No sirens or yelling, and the girl was still out on the backseat.

He drove home, thinking sooner or later he would see flashing lights in his rear view mirror and he would have to pull over. Then he pulled into his driveway. He'd done it!

The girl was still lying down on the seat as he drove into his garage and closed the door behind them, but she was slowly coming to. As he jumped out of the car, he picked up some duct tape from the work bench, and opening the door into the house, he put some on the girl's mouth and then on her wrists, keeping them together.

Richard then carried her to his old bedroom, placing her on the floor as he went to raise the concealed door. Once it was open, he went back to the girl who now looked panicked, and he forced her to go down the steps he had so carefully dug, pushing her along. He'd put a door into the room with a spy hole so that she couldn't surprise him when he came down the steps, but it was open now, so he pushed her inside and closed the door behind them. Now it was safe.

He pushed her onto the bed, and she held herself as best as she could in a fetal position, as he took off the duct tape.

"My dad will pay you whatever you want," she said defiantly, in her small voice.

"I don't want his money baby, it's you I want. And if you want to get out of here alive, then you do as I say. Now, take off your clothes, and I promise I'll be gentle."

CHAPTER 11

The couple who had disposed of Jane Doe and picked up Ashley and Sandy were on the road yet again.

Like virtually everyone else they knew, they were convicted sex offenders and so had to be extremely careful. The slightest mistake, they would be in trouble again, and although they had served their time, they still had many restrictions.

The woman, a very attractive lady who was actually older than Ashley had thought, had once had a normal family life with a husband and two children. A boy and a girl. Her husband had provided, they had a good life, no hardships, and the children grew up with everything they needed. She would watch her children play with their friends in the pool, and the house always seemed to be a hive of activity with kids coming and going.

It was never any problem until one of her son's friends began to pay her too much attention. She knew that her son's friends liked to look at her, her well-formed breasts and good legs made sure of that, but one kid pushed the envelope.

He would always tell her, out of earshot of the other kids, how beautiful she was, how he fantasized about her, and how he wanted her to teach him about sex. He looked at her all the time, and he was so smooth and slim, always staring at her. One day, finding herself alone with him, she invited him to her bedroom.

He promised he would never tell anyone as she taught him how to please her. His recovery rate was phenomenal compared to her husband, and he was always eager to learn, and to satisfy. Then it came crashing down. She had no idea how, but when she found herself in court and the boy was mouthing, "I'm sorry," while he was also sending her to prison, she couldn't believe she'd done anything wrong. It lost her everything. Nobody visited her in prison, no letters from her family or 'friends', only one letter from the boy himself, who said he was sorry again, especially for having bragged about his sexual learning to his best friend. He didn't want to testify against her, no harm had been done to him, and he was envied now by all his other friends. But she had been convicted of rape of a minor, and had to serve her time.

Now, she would only have sex with captive young boys. She did like to teach them, and these young boys wouldn't be able to tell tales that would get her re-arrested. The funny part for her was that she was now genuinely raping, but no one would ever convict her for it just because someone bragged about it.

The man she worked with was very different. He'd been a rapist of young girls who didn't want to be raped, although he was of the opinion they did. He thought all women wanted to be raped, but especially the young ones. Although the woman worked with him, she didn't like him, and he would have raped her if she'd been younger, as he thought she needed it.

He was only out of prison because most of his victims wouldn't testify against him. They didn't want to have to face him in court and be humiliated by his defense attorney, and they were very scared of him.

So now he was out, taking advantage of the captives. It was far from perfect for him, but it was safe.

Neither the man nor the woman went by their real names, so they called themselves Joe and Kirsty, which was the woman's daughter's name.

Joe was as mean looking as he acted. He always had a stubble, his white skin marked by scars, pockmarks, and tattoos. Irregular teeth stained yellow from smoking, his black hair cut close to his scalp, his nose bent from being broken.

They worked between Las Vegas and San Francisco, and sometimes Los Angeles. The house in San Francisco was mainly populated by Chinese boys, and the L.A. house by Mexicans. Joe and Kirsty didn't supply them, they specialized in getting the white kids and African Americans.

On this trip they had to go to Los Angeles first, who wanted three white girls, about thirteen or fourteen years old, attractive but not fat. They didn't care if they were blonde, brunette, redhead, or yellow. They needed to let three older girls go and wanted their replacements in place. It was a rush job, a client had placed an order, and Joe was very excited about it as he'd been told he could start the process on the girls, but not to mark them and to only have them anally.

Joe didn't care one way or the other about how he raped, he liked it both ways, and now he was being given three girls.

After checking their supplies, Kirsty and Joe left Las Vegas and made their way south to Phoenix. Three girls was going to be a challenge to them, the most they ever did was two, and Kirsty really didn't like the look of anticipation on her partner's face. Normally, they weren't allowed to touch the kids until they got to their destination, so Kirsty rarely saw or heard the young children being physically abused. She thought it was different with her boys, as she was teaching them and they rarely if ever screamed. But the girls..........

Joe and Kirsty spent the night on the outskirts of Phoenix, in a motel they paid for with cash and were asked no questions. Joe would have happily shared a room and a bed with Kirsty, but knew she wouldn't, so they got a room each. It wasn't exactly the height of luxury, prison seemed more hygiene, but it was a bed, and they were able to shower the following morning.

Kirsty disguised herself before they left the motel, very early the next morning, by pinning up her hair and donning a black wig. Altering her eye color with contact lenses, very different make up than what she normally used, and putting on a cream panted suit, she looked very much like the business woman, which was her intention. She also wore very large eye glasses that masked much of her face, and a floral silk scarf around her neck that hid her not unattractive mole.

Even though he'd seen the disguise before, Joe still did a double take as she exited her room with her bag, and as she got into the van, he returned the keys to the motel office.

There had at least been coffee machines in their rooms, but they were both hungry, and they stopped within a few minutes at the nearby Denny's.

After breakfast, Joe and Kirsty cruised around the city, looking for locations that were out of the way but only a short walk from the main mall. Once they'd decided, they set about their plan.

Leaving Joe, Kirsty made her way to the mall and headed directly to the food court. There, she bought herself a large mocha, and sat at a table pretending to work on the laptop that she'd taken out of her bag, but all the while she was watching, and waiting.

There were several opportunities, but not being quite right she bided her time. That is until three giggly girls sat down just a couple of tables away from her. They looked like the right age, neither of them was fat, and they were all very pretty.

Gathering up her stuff, Kirsty made her way over to them, and standing by the fourth chair at the table which was empty, introduced herself.

"Good morning. My name is Elizabeth Cromwell and I'm a senior associate at Ferndale Advertising Agency. I don't know if you've ever heard of us, but we represent clients like Clean Skin, James's Fashions, Dark Night Chocolates, Wondrous Laundry, Julian's Hair Products and many others." She handed out the business cards to confirm her identity, which the girls looked at and seemed convinced. "Do you mind if I sit with you for a minute?"

The girls all said no.

Sitting down, Kirsty retrieved a folder from her bag and continued talking.

"I'm only here today because we are taking photos of some young girls, just like yourselves, and I had a couple of hours to waste before they arrive. It's a local modeling agency that puts them forward to us, Nancy's they are called. Have you heard of them or seen their studio?"

The girls looked at each other, excitement in their eyes as they nodded and said it was just across the street.

"That's right," agreed the smiling Kirsty. "Anyway, what we are doing is shots like these." She handed out the glossy photos from her folder of face shots of young girls. The three girls passed them around to each other.

"Like I was saying. I was just in here having a coffee and catching up on a couple of things when I saw you girls arrive, and if you'll permit me, you are all very attractive and have great skin. Which is important because the shoot today is for a new face cream for teenagers, made by Clear Skin, and I wondered if we could take your photos before the other girls arrive. I must warn you that in all probability you all wouldn't be chosen, but we do want three girls, and if any of you were picked, then you'd be part of the upcoming campaign. So it would be television adverts, magazines, and billboards.

It wouldn't take long to do the photos. We have make up girls waiting around like myself along with the photographer, and if you agree to do it we'll also give you some money for your time. Would you be interested?"

All three girls were nodding their heads, laughing, and making comments to each other like, "Wouldn't it be cool", "What's there to lose?" "Can you imagine Jenny's face?"

"How much money?" One asked.

"I'll give of you each fifty, right now. If you don't show up then it's my loss. If you do, you'll get another hundred and fifty each. If you were to get chosen, then you would earn a great deal more and probably get other photo assignments as well. It could even start a very lucrative career. It is also just face shots we want, no nudity or suggestive clothing. So would you like to do it?"

The girls agreed and Kirsty handed each of them a fifty dollar bill. She also gave them three forms and pens to fill in for their names and addresses, telephone numbers, email addresses, Facebook pages, and agreeing to have their photos taken.

"Okay, while you fill in the forms, I'll get on the phone and make my way over there. As soon as you've filled in the forms, come on over and we'll get you set up. Now, there isn't a lot of space over there so don't start calling everyone to come and watch, they'll just get in the way. Whatever photos we take we'll send you copies, and you never know. One or more of you could well be a big part of our new campaign. So come on over to the studio, you'll have fun, and you'll see how a real photo shoot is done."

Kirsty got up, got all her things together and was talking on the phone as she left the girls busily filling in the forms. They heard her saying to get everything ready, she had three very pretty girls coming over, and didn't want them to be waiting around.

The girls didn't know it, but there was no one in the modeling agency. It was still closed and locked up. Kirsty was talking to herself.

Kirsty was waiting by the front door, on the phone, by the side of a van that had the passenger door open, and she waved at them happily as they made their way down the quiet street.

They paid no heed of the van as they got close to Kirsty, or the open sliding door on the side, but as soon as they passed it, Joe jumped out with a gun in his hand, and Kirsty said firmly, "Be quiet and no harm will come to you. Now get in the van, and be quick about it."

Kirsty had pulled her own gun out for good measure, pointing it at the girls, who just stood there stunned, still holding their forms.

"I won't tell you again. Get in the damn van!" She ordered.

They did, beginning to cry as Joe followed them in and closed the door behind them. Kirsty took a good look around, picking up one of the forms that had been dropped, and closed the passenger door that had been left open to use as a shield from prying eyes. It seemed to have worked as nobody was yelling or running toward her.

It was extremely rare for Kirsty and Joe to take 'regular' girls, they usually looked for fostered or adopted kids who were looking to escape. This was far more dangerous for them, although they got more money for it.

She got into the driver's seat, turned on the engine, put it in drive, and drove away. She turned on the radio so that she wouldn't hear Joe, and kept her eyes on the wing mirrors to make sure no one was following them.

CHAPTER 12

The FBI had far from given up on Ashley and Sandy. They may well have disbanded the task force they had set up when they went missing, involving as many law enforcement agencies as they could round up, but they were still looking.

Human trafficking is very much a hidden crime in the U.S.A., as most people can't believe that slavery is alive and well in this day and age. Experts say that almost 35 million people are living as slaves, when you include forced labor, human trafficking, the sale and exploitation of children, and forced marriage. India still has the highest rates for forcing their female children into marriage, the vast majority of whom are very young teenagers.

Billions of dollars a year are garnered on the backs of the unfortunate people who are either forced into prostitution, or into unpaid labor. The most trafficking occurs in Thailand, Cambodia, Latin America, and Eastern Europe. It's estimated that up to 2 million people are smuggled around the world every year by traffickers, who are generally known as 'Snakeheads'. The children's ages range from six to nineteen, with an average of eleven years old. The numbers increase every year, and some people estimate the numbers to be almost double or treble. It is also estimated that at least 100,000 children are prostituted in the US each year, most of whom are home grown.

Parents in third world countries are often so poor they feel forced to put their children into prostitution as the money that one child can earn in a week will feed their whole family. Or they sell them for a flat fee, not knowing where their child is going to be taken or how they are going to be treated.

If the trafficked children are to be used sexually, and most are, especially the girls, they have to endure a breaking down period which may involve torture with invasive tools, gang rapes, and addictive drugs. Eventually, they are so dependent on their captors, or pimps, that they become hostile to any rescuers. How they were taken and what they've been forced to do, even their real identities, is completely forgotten.

Most of the 'Snakeheads', especially in the U.S., are gangs who are not only well organized, but also have very severe rules about loyalty. This makes it exceedingly difficult for law enforcement to destroy their operations.

The majority of the children who are taken in the U.S. are foster children, adopted, or from broken homes. Unhappy kids who just want something better, adventure, or just safety. When they are approached by nice looking people offering a fun trip, some money, drinks, drugs, or just an escape, they jump at the opportunity. Very often these children may have a history of running away, may be in a home where the parents just don't care, so no alarm bells are rung when they disappear. They don't get an Amber Alert, they just become another statistic.

Two of the federal agents that had first responded to Ashley and Sandy's abduction were very much still on the case. This was their full time job in the Violent Crimes Against Children Section of the FBI, looking for minors who had been taken against their will and forced into prostitution, free labor, or organ donors.

Special Agents Olivia Danville, who was also the Task Force Officer in Charge, and Jonathan Forrester, were based in San Francisco. They worked very closely with many other agents around the country, sharing information such as pictures of the missing, identity marks, DNA results, vehicles used, anything and everything they had.

Olivia was in her mid-thirties now, had joined the FBI on leaving college, and loved her job even though it was heartbreaking and very frustrating at times. Married with two very young girls, her husband worked from home as an illustrator and was very understanding about her career and very supportive. Despite being a mother, Olivia didn't carry an ounce of surplus weight and seemed very slight. Yet she could run like the wind and had yet to meet a man who could take her down. She kept her black hair short, her make up light on pleasant features that included green eyes on her roundish face, and generally wore a professional looking trouser suit.

Jonathan was a little younger than Olivia, but like her had joined the FBI after college. He had really wanted to pursue serial killers, but after being assigned he had grown into the job and now really enjoyed it. Jonathan was divorced now. His wife had become increasingly disenchanted with his hours and absences and had sought and found, another partner. There were no children, although Jonathan had learned that his ex was now pregnant, yet they hadn't been divorced for very long.

Jonathan was tall, and although Olivia wasn't short he towered over her and most everyone else. He was also well formed, and got a lot of attention from women who seemed to like not only his size, but also the scars on his face from getting into a fight with a knife wielding gang member. The scars seemed to add character to his otherwise bland face, and dark blonde hair.

Olivia had left her personal card with the parents of Ashley and Sandy, with instructions to call her anytime and about anything. They called sometimes, asking if there was any news, or if she thought they were still alive. It was tragic, and Olivia could only imagine what she would do if her own children went missing.

Olivia had heard about the three missing girls in Phoenix but wasn't involved in it, as she and Jonathan had been busy at the Oakland docks with a shipment of Chinese children that had been found. The ship's captain, who was Norwegian, was vehemently protesting his innocence and Olivia was inclined to believe him, but his Chinese crew were saying nothing. Neither was anyone on shore. The FBI knew full well which street gang was behind this, but the news about the children spread before they could spring a trap on the gang members. They'd brought in some of the gang, but they all demanded lawyers and refused to answer any questions.

The children themselves were a little more helpful and they managed to get some descriptions and names that they shared with the authorities in Hong Kong. They also revealed which crew members were in on it.

After consulting with the ship's captain, the authorities in Hong Kong, and the Immigration Service, ICE, the crew members were put back on the ship that was returning directly to Hong Kong. The children were flown back on a chartered flight from San Francisco, and the Chinese authorities would handle it all at their end. It wasn't a perfect solution, and not one that was usually taken, but in this case it was probably the right one. The Chinese authorities were ruthless with traffickers, who would soon wish they had been co-operative with the Americans.

CHAPTER 13

The three now violated and humiliated girls from Phoenix, were now ensconced in a store front operation in Los Angeles. The first floor sold books and had a coffee bar, but by entering a code on one of the 'Staff Only' doors, the customers were able to climb the stairs to spend their money on personal time with any of the captive children.

This particular location was run by one of the Mexican gangs, who usually only provided smuggled Mexican children, but a very wealthy man had asked for three white American girls and had been willing to pay a lot of money. They were only too willing to oblige.

The gang itself was one of the nastiest. Life meant very little to them, and they were prone to publicly hanging their enemies, to warn others off their territory.

Once the three girls arrived, they were systematically tortured with cattle prods, canes, and clamps, along with being dosed by heroin. The girls, Susan, Melody, and Gretchen, had screamed, yelled and even fought, but they were no match for the gang members. After Gretchen had one of her toes cut off they quickly quieted down apart from the sobbing. The threat was clear to them. Try to escape and bad things would definitely happen to them.

It was several days before they were ready for the customer, and after Gretchen had her toe removed they'd been kept well apart, at the mercy of the gang members whose only forbidden act was not to take their virginity. That had been checked on their arrival.

The man who had paid for them was well known to the authorities, but with a combination of luck, money, and hidden threats, had so far eluded arrest. Everyone from the FBI to the local police knew of him, but whenever he'd been arrested the victim's story changed, and he was soon on his way again, smirking all the way out of the door.

He was followed to the book store by Special Agent James Carter, a veteran of twenty years who really disliked him. The Special Agent also frowned on his colleagues who perpetually nicknamed him 'Prez' when they were winding him up, which was often.

The wealthy guy was called William Stone, a balding short man, overweight, who always seemed to have a sickly smile on his ruby lips. Just the sight of him made the Special Agent shiver and squirm.

He'd followed William Stone to the book store regularly, waiting outside as he went in then appearing much later with another new book or two. James never thought much of it, put it in his report, then followed him to the next place, which was generally back to his very large home by the beach in Malibu. James thought he only lived there because he could ogle all the young girls on the beach, and no doubt jack off to them.

On returning to the same book store the following day instead of a week, James got suspicious, and although he'd been instructed only to follow William Stone at a very safe distance, he got out of his car and entered the book store a few seconds after William. James couldn't find him anywhere.

James raced around to the back of the store, but the only thing he saw there was a white van that was just pulling out. Although William Stone wasn't the driver or the passenger, James made a note of the license plate and the tags, just in case.

Pissed with himself, James went back to his car after making sure that William Stone's Jaguar was still in the same place, made his notes and waited.

The previous day, William had stayed in the book store for almost three hours, which was fairly normal for him, and James himself was a book lover, who could easily spend an even longer time in a library. So James had never got suspicious.

Today, even though by now James was sure that William was somewhere else and up to no good, he surprised James by emerging from the book store with another book, still grinning that slimy smile of his.

William went straight home, and James, after following him there, went back to the book store for a better look around. James was positive that he'd been given the slip somehow. The only exit door apart from the front entrance was an emergency door that would set off an alarm if opened. James walked around some more and then noticed one of the staff only doors had a keypad, and a very discreet camera above the door. Grabbing a book off one of the many shelves, James found a seat where he could keep an eye on the door while pretending to read, and noticed there was a regular procession through the door. The ones going in tapped in a code, the ones coming out picked up a book and then paid for it at the front desk. James pretended to use his phone and snapped off a few pictures of the people using the door, sending them to his office. They weren't staff, he knew that, and he really wanted to get behind that door.

Not wanting to start looking suspicious himself, James put his book back, found one much more to his liking, and bought it before leaving the store. Once back in his car he called the office to see if the people in his photos were anyone of interest. He was told to return to the office as soon as someone relieved him at the bookstore, and he gave them his location in the car park.

On returning to the office, James was surprised to find a large evidence board was already in place, with pictures of all the people he'd photographed along with a very detailed plan of the book store. James's senior, Bob James, the Task Force Officer, was waiting for him.

"James, good work, what made you suspicious?" Asked Bob.

James told him his story and asked him who all the people were in the photos.

"Every last one of them is a pedophile. We're going in tomorrow, and hopefully William Stone will go back there as well. Now show me which door they use inside the book store and I'll go over with you what the plan is. This is great work James, but whatever is going on in there, we need to stop it before they realize we're on to them and disappear."

James didn't think for one minute that William Stone would go back to the book store the next day. He would probably go shopping, and James would miss the big bust. More pictures had been taken and crazy Mexican gang members had been identified coming out of the book store, without books, and everyone knew they would start shooting at the first sign of a bust. James didn't like gunfights, but anything was better than following the pervert William Stone around town.

Just after lunchtime, James spotted the Jaguar pulling out of the garage, and once it was a safe distance in front of him he followed, overjoyed when he parked up yet again at the book store car park.

James radioed in to tell them of his status, and he was instructed to go to the unmarked van in the parking lot, to prepare for the bust.

It was another hour before everyone was ready, and more pedophiles had entered the book store. A team was covering the rear, and a SWAT team was going in first. Everyone was aware that a gun fight was going to ensue, so no one was going in without body armor and plenty of ammunition. The ATF had a crew here, fire engines were positioned, paramedics were waiting around the corner, and once the SWAT team entered, the book store would be quickly emptied and everyone identified in a safe place, before they were released or arrested. Immigration also had people, along with child social services if there were indeed children inside. A warrant had been issued, so when Special Agent Bob James gave the order to "GO", everybody's weapon was drawn and they moved fast.

As soon as the SWAT team pulled up in their truck and swarmed into the book store, they were followed by regular police who quickly evacuated the book store and ran them to a nearby building to be processed.

Gunfire erupted very quickly, and the upper windows started smashing as straggling book store patrons ran for cover below. FBI agents followed the SWAT team, snipers covered the windows, and it was bedlam inside the building as they swept through from room to room, with rapid fire and stun grenades going off, ATF running up the stairs after the FBI, and then the sirens as the paramedics and the fire engines made their way over to the store.

The gunfire went on for over fifteen minutes. The gang members weren't for surrendering, and then the order went out for more ambulances, as paramedics were summoned up the stairs, along with child services and Immigration.

As the smoke cleared but the smell of cordite remained, it seemed to get even more chaotic as Crime Scene moved in, men in handcuffs were taken out, bodies on gurneys appeared and then were gone, and TV news crews had arrived, along with a clutch of reporters and photographers.

Inside, the details were beginning to emerge, slowly but surely as they all drew breath and compared notes, checking and re-checking the information.

Twenty two young girls, mainly Mexican but also three Caucasian were discovered, with ages ranging from approximately eight, to nineteen. There were also three young boys, of Mexican descent, who were aged between ten and thirteen. Three of the Mexican girls had been wounded, one seriously, and one of the boys was critical.

Twelve gang members were accounted for, ten were deceased, and two were on their way to hospital with critical wounds. Two of the twelve had been shot on the escape ladder at the back of the store, after firing on the FBI agents positioned at the rear, and were among the dead.

Ten suspected pedophiles had been arrested, four of them in compromising positions, two of them wounded and receiving treatment in hospital.

Three of the SWAT team had been wounded, one fatally, and two FBI agents had also been wounded, one in serious condition.

The children were now being processed by the FBI, Immigration, Doctors and Children's Social Services in hospital rooms. The bookstore was now roped off and not accessible, until Crime Scene collected evidence, which they estimated would take many days.

An APB had also been issued for the white van that Special Agent James 'The Prez' Carter had made a note of.

CHAPTER 14

Hui and Ning, were orphans in San Francisco who had run away from their foster home. Being continuously beaten, worked endlessly in the laundry, and given no money or any free time, had finally gotten to them. They weren't related, but became friends in the orphanage and were thrilled when they were sent to live with the same Chinese family in Chinatown. That was a year ago, and now they were living on the streets, dodging the police who would be sure to detain them, as they were only eleven years old.

Their hair had grown since escaping, and now it was dirty and limp. Both boys were very slight, small, but didn't look alike as they had very different noses and mouths. They'd tried to stay washed and neat on the streets, but it was difficult. Stores didn't like street kids using their restrooms, and the public ones were generally dangerous.

Some of the homeless adults had helped them out, but others were mean and foul mouthed, and didn't like kids encroaching on their territory. Most of the homeless had their own spots for begging, and they were very protective of them, so Hui and Ning were often chased away by knife wielding vagrants.

Any money they were able to scrounge, they spent on food, or on things to keep them warm and dry, which was no easy task in San Francisco.

When they were approached by a good looking man who was very well dressed, who told them he could give them a good life away from the streets, he got their interest. Telling them that they would have their own rooms, three good meals a day, nice clothing, warm beds, and a safe environment sounded like heaven to them.

When Ning asked what they would have to do in return, they were told it just entailed keeping people happy, getting them what they needed in a nice relaxed atmosphere. It was easy, nothing hard or strenuous, and when they learned the ropes, which wouldn't take long, they would make very good money.

Ning and Hui, looked at each other, and the man let them talk about it between themselves, taking a few steps away, so as not to pressure them.

"Will we be able to have rooms next to each other?" Ning asked loudly, to make sure the fellow Chinese man heard.

"Of course. There would be no reason to split you up, it looks like you've gone through a lot together. But staying on the street is no answer, it's too dangerous. Half of these people are mental cases, and they'd slit your throats for a couple of dollars. It's up to you guys. If you want to stay out here and take your chances I can't stop you. It's a free world. Or you come with me, we get you cleaned up, some new clothes, put some food into you, and your lives will change for the better."

Ning and Hui talked some more and agreed. They were tired, hungry, cold, and needed a better place than the park to sleep in.

The man, who said his name was Charlie, led the way and took them down Sacramento Street, past Chinatown, toward the bay. He then took a left turn and then the first right, so that they were now at the rear entrances of the properties on Sacramento. Stopping at a door beside a garage after taking a good look around, he knocked, and when the door opened he ushered the two boys inside, locking the door behind him.

The two boys world, that they'd just been so excited about, came to an abrupt end. They were met by four members of a Chinese gang that they knew about and had kept distance from. Even at their young age they'd heard stories about them, their penchant for using knives and guns, and the protection money they extorted from the local businesses.

The five men surrounded the boys in a parking bay next to a white van, and they were told to strip. Completely. They did as they were told then were tossed a large black refuse bag and instructed to put all their clothing in it, along with everything else they were carrying. They wanted to keep some things but weren't allowed to, and then they were each given a bar of antibacterial soap. After being told to wash every inch of their skins, from head to foot, twice, someone turned on a hose and they were sprayed with cold water, everybody making sure they did as they were told. The shivering Ning and Hui were then ordered to stand facing the wall, to bend over and touch the wall with their hands, and keep their legs apart. Then they were raped.

The day before, three young Mexican girls who'd been bought from Los Angeles had arrived, and even though they were already schooled, they also went through the same process. The Chinese would do business with the Mexicans, but they didn't trust them, and they liked to enforce their own initiation.

Once they were finished with the two boys, they made them wash again before giving them towels and some new clothes.

Escorting the boys upstairs, the crying Ning asked Charlie about his promises to them.

"Kid, we own you now. Do as you're told and you'll get to like it. You won't starve, you'll have a nice bed to sleep in, and when we let you go you'll have a well-paid career. If you don't behave, these guys will cut you up. So stay wise kid."

They were taken to their rooms, not next door to each other, drugged, and then caged. It was a tried and tested routine, and very rarely failed.

As the two boys were being caged, Kirsty and Joe were getting the van ready. They were delivering a Chinese boy to someone in San Jose who had purchased him from the house, and then they were going to head back to Las Vegas, via Fresno. There they would try to find an unhappy orphan or two. Nobody had told them yet about Los Angeles, and as they couldn't understand the excited chatter that was going around, they left.

They had barely left the city on the 101 when a highway patrol was flashing its lights behind them, and was waiting for them to pull over.

The cop in his cruiser kept them waiting for a long time before wandering down to the driver's window and asking Kirsty for her driver's license and insurance. He didn't reply when she asked if they'd done something wrong. Instead, he just retreated back to his car and took his seat again in front of the dashboard computer.

Kirsty and Joe knew they could be in trouble, but they couldn't outrun the cop in the van so the only other option was to kill him when he returned, so that his dash camera wouldn't get their faces. Or maybe he wouldn't realize the driver's license and insurance was fake, and just hand them a ticket for whatever he pulled them over for. Kirsty got her gun out ready, concealing it behind the driver's door.

As the cop finally emerged, watched closely in the wing mirror by Kirsty to see if he was pulling his gun, the cop was passed by two black suburbans who braked at the last moment, blocking the van in, and then there were seven people, including the cop, who were pointing guns at Kirsty and Joe, shouting at them to show their hands.

With a look of resignation at Joe, Kirsty tried to hide her gun behind the seat she was sitting in before raising her hands, Joe doing likewise with his weapon and then his hands. Once their hands were in clear view, both doors were opened for them and they were told to exit the vehicle, keeping their hands in visible.

Kirsty mentioned her seat belt was still on, so she was told to unclip it very slowly with just one hand, and then raise it again before getting out of the vehicle. Joe was told to wait until she'd excited the vehicle before doing the same thing.

Once they were out of the van, they were told to place their hands on the side of the hood, and spread their legs to be searched.

Asked if they had any weapons on them they both said no, which they repeated when asked if they had any weapons in the vehicle. They also said no when they were asked if anyone else was in the vehicle.

After being searched from head to toe, Joe and Kirsty were cuffed and were led over to the side of the road and told to sit down, which they did.

"Are we under arrest?" Asked Joe.

"Quite possibly," replied Special Agent Danville.

"Have you got a search warrant for that?" Asked Joe again, as agents started looking into the van.

"Yes sir," replied Special Agent Danville, who produced the piece of paper from a pocket and showed it to Joe.

The special agent was called over to the van that had produced not only the two handguns, but also a restrained young boy in the rear, an address on the GPS system on the dashboard, a laptop, briefcase, luggage, wigs, along with a small bag of hyperthermia needles, and vials of some kind of substance.

"We need to get this van towed back a.s.a.p. and have forensics go over it with a fine tooth comb," she instructed, "and someone read those two their rights. Tell them they are being arrested for illegal concealment of firearms and suspected kidnapping of a minor, along with possession of illegal narcotics."

Special Agent Danville was quite happy as she made her way back to the office, and she wondered what else they would find out about the couple driving the van, and of the van itself.

CHAPTER 15

In Dallas, Texas, a huge manhunt had been going on for the missing rich girl, and although it was abating now, it was still making the news albeit in much shorter bulletins. Richard Brand had opened his door to many cops who were looking for the young girl, even letting them look around his home without a warrant, and none of them had found his secret cellar.

As his neighbors watched from inside their fences, thinking they'd be finally rid of their unwanted pervert, Richard would smile at them all from his front yard, as his property was searched again and again. Richard wasn't the only one. All the sex offenders in a fifty mile radius were being harassed, but no sign of the girl had been found anywhere.

Although Richard didn't have any friends anymore, if he had they would have noticed how much happier he was. His only regret was that he hadn't done it earlier. Much earlier.

He especially enjoyed the very first encounter when the girl had fought him as he tore her clothes off. Since then, she had become more and more compliant as he taught her what he liked.

His most dangerous task was getting clothes for her, for his own amusement. His favorite was the school uniform with a short skirt, or the French maid's, so he'd managed to get them from a store he knew about and paid for them with cash.

But Richard Brand wasn't the only one keeping a secret in the huge state of Texas. During the manhunt other undocumented kids had been found in sex offender's homes or properties. Mexicans smuggled over the border, or kids who had been previously classed as runaways. And that was just in the Dallas/Fort Worth region.

Elsewhere in Texas, from San Antonio to Houston and beyond, other kids were in dire straits, either having to work seven days a week from morning to night, or being used for sex or both.

Undocumented adults were also being used. If they weren't working as prostitutes, then they were used as labor, watched over by the armed gangs who would kill at the slightest provocation. All these people had wanted was a new life out of Mexico, and in searching for help in getting over the border, had fallen into the hands of the gangs who had different plans for them. They went from one hell to another, and it was difficult to determine which was worse.

Two girls, daughters of parents who were now working in hot fields for nothing, had been sold to a particularly nasty man in Austin. Apart from raping, he liked to inflict pain, and the more screams he could elicit from the victims the better he liked it. Eventually, he would go too far and then he would contact the gang again for two more girls, starting the process all over again.

The gang knew full well what he was about, that he was a serial killer as well as a pedophile, but they had no remorse whatsoever in selling the kids to him. As far as they were concerned, it was just business. His money was as good as anyone else's.

It was very lucrative for the traffickers. They could sell everyone but the old and the infirm, singly or in groups. The highest demand was of course for the children, and once they took their photos and dressed them up a little, the prices shot up.

Some people didn't like dealing with the gangs and they would go into Mexico to find their own, taking the risk of smuggling them back themselves. They would even talk to their parents and tell them lie after lie about how they would give their children a good education in return for a few simple chores around the house.

Others would hand over cash to the parents, then would believe that they owned the child as if they had bought a pet. Slavery wasn't dead. It was positively thriving.

CHAPTER 16

As more and more time passed, Ashley and Sandy got deeper into the hole. Already they were living for the next hit, and taking care of the customers got them there sooner. If they were surly or uncooperative, then their injection was delayed until they made up for it, so they learned to show pleasure to the customers, or pain if that was what they required.

Most of the time they were in a daze. They didn't recall how they had been brought here, wherever here was, and had no memory left of their families or their real names. When they came across each other, it wasn't as best friends, it was just someone else in their pajamas, being given food just like themselves.

The personnel was always changing. Different faces, different colors, different languages. It didn't matter to Ashley or Sandy, nobody really talked about anything apart from the story on the soap operas that were always on the TV. The main thing was when the next injection was.

When Ashley was sold on, Sandy never even noticed.

Ashley was sold to a local pimp who usually took the older girls after they'd served their purpose in the hotel. He was a good customer, so when he asked if any of the younger girls were available, Ashley was suggested as new girls had already been ordered.

The pimp wasn't a nice guy but he had access to drugs that he would need to keep Ashley compliant. The first thing he did was rape her and beat her up, telling her that would keep happening if she didn't do as she was told. In return, he would look after her, keep her from nasty customers, and if someone did treat her badly, then he would take care of them permanently.

He scared Ashley half to death, but once she recovered from the beating he kept to his word, and she saw firsthand the punishment he meted out to customers who wanted to slap her around. He also promised her that once she'd paid back his debt she would earn very good money, but until then, she was his property. Ashley didn't really care. She just wanted her regular fix.

The hotel had found two new drivers to find and pick up the kids. They'd heard about the arrest of Joe and Kirsty very quickly, as well as the raid on the bookstore in L.A. It wasn't a huge shock, it was always happening, and resources were available to carry on in different places, with new personnel, as if nothing had happened.

Already, a new location was in use in L.A., and it was business as usual.

Kirsty and Joe had lawyered up as soon as they were arrested. Even if they agreed to plea deal with the FBI, the lawyer who was provided by the gangs would inform his employer, and if he even thought they would go down that road, photos would be provided of anyone in Joe and Kirsty's life, to let them know that they wouldn't be safe.

Special Agent Danville was well aware of this, but no amount of promises of protection was good enough. It was very rare when an employee turned, they were always too scared to do so. They would rather be taken care of back in prison, with a lot of protection, which was very important to child molesters.

The boy that they'd found tethered in the rear of the van had yet to be of any use. He was having to go through therapy and drug rehabilitation, and like most victims, he was now hostile with the people trying to help him.

There was no record of him, no name, no nothing, and it was like he didn't exist.

The van was turning up all kinds of information despite it being well cleaned. Not only did it contain Ashley and Sandy's partial fingerprints, but also a deceased woman's DNA in Brentwood, and one of the three girls that were taken from Phoenix. Those three girls were the good news.

When they were found in the book store, they had all been violated, raped, and drugged, but they weren't as far along as most of the victims. Their therapy and rehab wouldn't take as long, and they still knew their families and real names.

The L.A. office were already saying that the girls would be capable of identifying the couple who had picked them up, and they would also be able to testify against the elusive William Stone, who'd been caught naked with one of the three girls with a lot of evidence to use against him.

The couple arrested in the van had their own histories. Both had been convicted of child molestation and rape. Now they faced charges of illegal possession of concealed guns, using aliases, violating parole, kidnapping, rape, and possibly murder. Not to mention being in the wrong state, the heroin, and having a captive child in the back of their vehicle, which was stolen and had false plates.

Although there was no information about the child, he had the teeth and body development of a twelve year old. The couple were looking at a lot of years, probably life, behind bars.

Special Agent Danville was putting the most pressure on the guy who owned the address on the van's GPS system. So far he was denying any involvement, but he knew more than he was saying, so they were gaining leverage about him.

CHAPTER 17

Bec's life in New Jersey wasn't getting any easier with the McGrady's. Bec was still pretending not to know any English, so when the McGrady's got into a spat, they did so quite openly in front of her.

Mrs. McGrady's biggest gripe was that her husband was spending too much time with Bec, especially when she was out of the house, and that they seemed to have got their priorities wrong. Mrs. McGrady was saying that with the other girls they'd had, they'd been as more of an appetizer before the main course, which was each other. Now, her husband was spent when she was horny, and it wasn't working. She liked Bec making her orgasm, but then she wanted some cock, and it wasn't being provided.

Mr. McGrady kept apologizing, but he was blaming Bec for being too good at sex, and that before he knew it, and before he could pull away, it had gotten too late.

Bec knew full well he was telling his wife lies. When the wife wasn't around, he would say things that he didn't think Bec could understand, about his controlling wife who was getting worse, and how much better the sex was with a young nubile girl, who didn't nag all the time.

Mrs. McGrady was believing her husband, and then she was pushing Bec out of the door and tying her to the tree again.

The only logical conclusion that Bec could think what would eventually happen to her, would be thrown onto the streets somewhere, or killed. Even if she started talking and told Mrs. McGrady that her husband didn't like her anymore, that he thought she was too bossy and he didn't like being ordered about, she felt she would still be thrown out. Or probably worse. As she shivered under the tree, Bec was thinking she would have to run, but didn't know which direction to take. She had no idea where she was, or where to go, or who to look for. Escaping was the easy part. It was the rest that scared her.

As she contemplated what to do, a neighbor was on his roof repairing a loose slate, and he noticed Bec tied to the tree. He wasn't close to his neighbors, they might say hello on seeing each other, but they never chatted although he knew they didn't have children. So the girl in the yard wasn't their daughter. Even if they'd fostered or adopted her, people just don't tie their children to a tree on a cold day, or at any other time.

As he sat on his roof, he got his cell phone out of his pocket and called 911, telling the operator his name and address before saying it wasn't an emergency, but his next door neighbors had tied a young girl to a tree in their back yard, and he was worried about her.

The operator told him to stay on the phone, asked for the house number of next door's house, and that a patrol car was on its way. The operator asked how he'd managed to see the girl so he explained, and was told to remain there until the patrol car arrived, but if the situation changed, to say so. So he remained on his roof, wondering if he'd done the right thing, until the patrol car pulled up and he waved at them as the two cops got out of the car.

The neighbor told the operator that the cops had arrived and had gone to his neighbors front door, confirming that the girl was still in the same place. A moment later, the two cops were with the couple who owned the house, exiting the rear of the house. He was told then to vacate his roof and wait outside the front of his house. The operator thanked him for his help and hung up on him.

Doing as he was told, thinking he was going to be charged with wasting the police's time, he waited, wondering what the innocent explanation was and how he was going to explain this to his wife.

Very soon, more vehicles began to arrive and people were entering the house, which really got the neighbor's attention, and then a woman came up his drive. She introduced herself as a detective, asked him to give a statement of what he'd witnessed, so he took her inside.

The detective wasn't very forthcoming on what was going on, but when she left, passing his wife on the driveway, the couple from next door were being escorted out of their house in handcuffs, and put into two separate cars.

An hour later, after telling his wife what had happened but still remaining on their driveway, a couple came over from next door, identified themselves as FBI Special Agents, and asked if they could go into their house to talk some more. It was only then that the neighbor and his wife learned that their next door neighbors were suspected of keeping a girl against her will, for free labor and for sexual favors, and the FBI wanted to know how long the girl had been there.

"You mean that girl has been kept next door as a slave?" The shocked man asked.

"We believe so."

"Oh my God!" The man gasped, "I had no idea. This is just awful."

The neighbor and his wife hugged each other as they learned of what had been going on just steps away from them.

"Actually, we came here to thank you for noticing something wasn't right and for calling 911. Most people in your position would have just ignored it. You did the right thing sir, so thank you. Now if you wouldn't mind, can we just go over again what exactly happened today?" One of the agents asked.

"Of course. This is just incredible!"

As the neighbor went over his story again, Bec was taken away by Child Services and another FBI agent for a medical examination. The house was now a crime scene and it was being processed by a forensics team.

As Bec knew English, she was very helpful in as much as she could. She was certainly instrumental in building the case against the McGrady's, and she was even able to tell the FBI where the couple kept their secret papers. The McGrady's were heading to prison for a long time, no matter how much information they gave about purchasing Bec, and who from.

Bec herself was going to go through therapy. She would be allowed to stay in the USA, but during her medical examination, it was discovered she was pregnant. She was given legal representation to help her sue the McGrady's for her ordeal and condition, but the decision about the baby wasn't an easy one, and it was left for Bec to decide on it when she was mentally stable.

CHAPTER 18

Lexie was a thirteen year old girl in a foster home in Portland, Oregon. It was her third foster home, and her foster father thought it was his right to be able to touch her in intimate places.

This was the third foster home that Lexie had been placed in, because she was classed as a troublemaker, and a disruptive influence on other foster children. Lexie herself didn't think so, she just didn't like being sent to homes where in her opinion, they only fostered for the money. Lexie knew that all foster parents weren't like that, it was only a tiny minority, but she'd never felt cared for in any of the homes she'd been to.

When she was called a troublemaker, or a disruptive influence, it was because she defended the younger children who she thought deserved better. Lexie had witnessed the younger ones being beaten and abused, given no guidance on anything, yet were punished for doing wrong. The foster parents would drink, only buy basic food for a little as possible, and would send the kids to their shared rooms after their evening meal. Lexie thought life was better in the orphanage than in the homes she'd been sent to, such had been her experience.

Lexie herself was a pretty girl, but had taken to wearing black clothing and black make up. She wasn't supposed to wear makeup, so she would apply it on leaving the house, and the pupils at the school she was currently going to, called her a witch. Beneath the oversized clothing, she was slim, had long black hair, green eyes, and a great smile that was seldom seen.

One night, when everyone was asleep, Lexie crept down the stairs with all her worldly belongings contained in a backpack, and put it by the front door which she unlocked. She then found the purse that was left by the foster mother in the living room by a couple of empty glasses, and took what cash was in there. Then, seeing the laptop that was off limits to the children, Lexie opened it and found it was just sleeping. If it had been turned off, Lexie probably wouldn't have been able to do anything with it, as she didn't know the password. Finding the website for the orphanage, she wrote them a comment saying the foster parents were drunks, the man was always groping the girls, and life for the children was hellish. After leaving the address of the home, she logged off and left the house.

Lexie made her way to the bus station, which was quite a walk, and she kept her eyes open for cops who would probably pick her up if they saw her.

Lexie didn't know where to head to, she just wanted to get away, but the cash in her pocket dictated how far she could go. The only fare she could afford, leaving a little for some food, was the BoltBus to Seattle.

After buying the ticket, there was some time to spare, so Lexie had a small breakfast from a nearby cafe, not worrying about cops now because it was light and the city had woken up.

It was a three hour bus ride to Seattle, so Lexie caught up on some sleep as she wondered what she would do when she got there.

Arriving in Seattle, Lexie was approached by a pleasant young man, about twenty five years old, who asked her if she was okay, if she needed any help, or if she had a place to go to and food to eat.

Lexie passed him off, politely, and for the next few hours wandered around aimlessly, wondering what she'd got herself into. It was quite cold in Seattle, and she began to think of where she would be able to sleep and to keep warm. She was also getting hungry. As it began to get dark, Lexie returned to the bus station.

Sitting on one of the fixed seats, Lexie tried to make herself comfortable thinking she would be spending the night there, and although it wasn't warm, it was out of the cold air and bearable.

She was there for about an hour before the same young man from before sat down beside her.

"Hey, I'm Jess. Are you okay?"

"I'm fine," Lexie replied.

"If you need help, all you need to do is say so."

"I'll be okay," said the unconvincing Lexie.

"Listen. I'm hungry so I'm going to grab a burger. Can I get you one?" He asked.

"No, I'll be fine. You go ahead."

"It's my treat. You look starved. You want fries with it?"

"Okay then, sure. I'll have fries as well Jess."

Jess left Lexie in the bus station and she wondered if he would return. She thought he was pretty good looking with his stubble and wayward brown hair, and seemed like a normal guy in his jeans, tee shirt, and short wool coat.

Jess was back ten minutes later.

"Here you go," he said, handing Lexie a bag and sitting down next to her. "I got you a hot chocolate as well. Seemed a bit too chilly for coke."

"Thanks," replied the thankful Lexie, taking the bag and the drink. "My stomach was beginning to rumble a bit."

Putting the hot drink to one side, she opened the bag to find the burger was in a cardboard container, so when she opened it, there was a place to put the fries. Doing that, she took the napkins and ketchup out of the bag, placed the bag under the container, then opened one of the ketchups, squeezing out the contents to dip her fries in.

They both sat there quietly, eating, until they'd finished, and Jess took their remnants and dropped them in the garbage can, as Lexie took a sip of her chocolate.

"So what brings you to Seattle? You got family here?" He asked.

"No, I just needed to get away from where I was at is all."

"You were in a bad place?" Jess enquired.

"Yeah, you could say that"

"Won't your parents be worried about you? They've probably got the police involved, so I could go and find one if you like and they'll see you'll get home safe."

"I don't have any parents. I was in a foster home and they don't care. They'll only go to the police if it hurts their pocket. That's all they care about."

"I'm sorry, that really sucks. What's your name by the way?"

"Lexie."

"So do you have anywhere to go to Lexie, some friends here or anything?" I could give them a call if you want."

"No, but I'll be okay. I'll spend the night here and then get myself organized in the morning."

"It's pretty dangerous around here for young girls who are alone. Listen. I have a pal who could put you in a motel room for the night and it's not far from here. At least you'll have a bed and some warmth for the night, and then you can decide what to do after a good night's sleep."

"Why would your friend want to help me, and why do you?" Asked the suspicious Lexie. "I can't afford to go to a motel."

"It's right that you ask that Lexie, and very sensible of you. We hear and read a lot of stories about young people who come to the city and get picked up by the wrong people. Me and my friends talk about it a lot and what would we do if we noticed a young person who seemed to be all alone. It was only talk but we thought we would like to help if we could. I was here earlier to meet an old friend and I noticed you, offered you some help but you declined. I thought someone was going to meet you. When I had to come back down here tonight to drop something off, I thought I would make sure you'd gone someplace so that I wouldn't worry about you. But here you are, and now I will probably worry about you all night."

"There's no need to worry about me Jess, I can take care of myself."

"I'm sure you can Lexie, but I know my friend will give you a bed. He won't expect you to pay him, we just couldn't bear to think of you all alone in here. Tell you what Lexie. You have a think about it and I'll go and wait for you by the entrance doors over there," he pointed. "I'll wait ten minutes, but if you prefer to take your chances around here so be it, you can just stay put. I"Lel head home, knowing that at least I tried to help, but I can't force you to do the right thing. So I'll go now, and if you want to come that'll be great. If you don't, I understand, and I wish you well. Okay?"

"Okay Jess. Let me think for a while, but thank you for the food and the drink, they were great."

"You're welcome Lexie. Take care of yourself."

Jess left Lexie sipping the last of her hot chocolate and waited outside, checking the time on his watch, zipping up his coat and putting his hands in his pockets to keep them warm. When nine minutes had passed, Lexie joined him and he took her on the short walk to the motel, which was by no means a top of the range resting place. It was just one level with all the rooms set in an upside down U, and no one could enter or leave without passing the motel's office.

Jess left Lexie outside the office as he went inside, and spoke to a big bald black man. At one point, the bald man came outside, looked around, looked at Lexie, went back inside and talked some more with Jess before handing over a couple of things to him. They shook hands, and then Jess came back outside.

"Okay Lexie, you're all set up. My friend is very happy to give you a room for the night, so let me show you where it is."

The friend didn't look that happy to Lexie but she followed Jess to her room.

Opening the door with the key he'd been given, turning on the lights, he gave Lexie a very short tour of the bathroom, the microwave, coffee machine, how to use the heater, and how to operate the TV. The bed was huge in Lexie's eyes, a king size, and although the room smelt a little funny, everything seemed clean and the towels weren't too thin.

Jess handed her the door key, told her to lock it behind him, and to get a good night's sleep. Lexie thanked him for his help as he left, closed the drapes, turned up the heat, put the TV on and lay on the bed that was surprisingly comfortable. After a few minutes, she got undressed to her underwear, pulled the covers down, and got into bed. She fell asleep with the TV and bedside light still on, in the very plain but functional room.

It was about an hour later and Lexie was being woken up by the big black man from the motel office. He spoke with a very deep voice and he was as scary as hell.

"Hey, wake up girl," he bellowed, repeating himself until Lexie shot up.

"I've just paid a lot of money for you girl, so it's time you started paying me back. Take off your panties."

"What do you mean? Paid a lot of money for me? I don't understand you," replied the very frightened Lexie.

"Your ass was just sold to me for a thousand bucks so I own you now girl, until you can pay me back with interest. If you don't, you die, to whoever pays the most to kill you. I know a lot of weird guys who would pay very well to kill you, and it wouldn't be painless. So let me tell you how this works girl. I tell you what to do and who with, and I look after you. Nobody hurts you or I hurt them, and worse. Until I can trust you, you don't go anywhere without me or one of my friends. You'll be fed and clothed, but there is nowhere for you to run to. I will find you and you will pay. Now do you understand girl? I now own you."

Lexie could only nod, she was shaking so much.

"Open the drawer girl and pass me one of the packets. You don't let anyone not use one, you understand?"

Lexie nodded again and opened the drawer on the nightstand that was filled with condoms in various colors and sizes.

"I need a large one," he said, "and take your underwear off."

Lexie found one marked L and took the rest of her clothes off, trying to hide her private parts behind her hands.

"Lay back on the bed girl, this will hurt the first time but then you'll like it."

Lexie cried as he got undressed.

CHAPTER 19

Things weren't looking good for the man in San Jose, who'd been expecting a young boy to be delivered to him. From eagerly looking forward to his delivery, instead he had the FBI rapping on his door, and he was put in handcuffs and taken to their offices in San Francisco.

Michael Wilson was already a convicted pedophile. He'd been attracted to children for as long as he could remember, especially boys, but he had married and tried to not think about it. He and his wife had even had their own children, a boy and a girl. Then somehow, he couldn't recall when, he started looking at child porn, and it culminated in him making a date online with a boy, who had allowed him to have sex with him for a fee. After that, he would have sex with older boys who were prostituting themselves on the streets, but then went back online for a younger boy and got stung.

He still cursed himself for going to that home where supposedly the boy lived, going inside and getting filmed before being arrested. Since then, he'd lost his wife and children who wanted nothing more to do with him, he had feared for his life in prison, and was now a registered sex offender.

Michael was now middle aged, a short man with greying brown hair that was parted down the side, a slight paunch from sitting too much, and looks that would be best described as blotchy. He'd been plagued by poor skin for years, with red marks on his cheeks and forehead. When he was younger, it was described as rosy cheeked, but with age, it just looked a little odd, or that he'd been caught in the sun.

He was an accountant by profession, so he always had work, but he'd never been 'cured' as he liked to put it, of his attraction to children. He'd saved his money to get one of his own, and now, before he'd had chance to take advantage, the FBI had arrived and he knew he was going back to prison.

Michael lawyered up on being arrested. He thought it was his only hope, but as the evidence mounted against him, the less hopeful he became. He'd rented his home in San Jose because it had a back yard that was grassed, but hidden behind it was a previous tenants vegetable patch with a shed. He didn't attempt to revitalize the vegetable garden, but he had worked on the shed, and whenever the parole officers came around, they had never seen the shed. He had planned on putting the boy in there, but the FBI found it, along with all his illegal magazines stored inside.

Special Agent Danville knew they had Michael Wilson over a barrel, but she wanted to know where the boy had been transported from. The boy himself was still out of it and probably wouldn't know anyway, and the two from the van were resolute in not saying anything. There was no way the Special Agent would give them a deal to keep either of them out of prison, so it was a stalemate. As far as the Special Agent was concerned, they could rot there.

She would though do a deal with Michael Wilson. It was just a matter of what his lawyer would agree to before persuading his client. He would still have to do time, but she could make it easier for him with the right establishment and much less time than he was presently looking at. But first she had to establish if he knew where the boy had been kept, what kind of operation it was, and how many children there were.

So there was a lot of negotiating. Michael Wilson didn't want to give too much away and the Special Agent wouldn't agree to a deal unless his information was good and would lead to many convictions.

However, once Michael admitted that he knew where the location was, without implicating himself by saying he'd had sex in there, the deal was made and the Special Agent had her address. Gallingly, it was very near to the FBI office in San Francisco.

Immediately, the building was put on a round the clock surveillance with agents in nearby buildings filming the comings and goings, vehicles followed, and people identified.

Special Agent Danville put her team together. All the agents she could muster, U.S. Marshals, ICE, ATF, and the local police along with a SWAT team. She would have preferred to go in at the crack of dawn, and hopefully avoid the shooting that happened in L.A., but there would be no customers then and she really wanted to catch them in the act. Just knowing who the customers were wasn't good enough, as the kids were usually so far out of it they couldn't testify against anyone. So she decided to go in when several customers had entered the house. Quickly, before anyone had time to think.

Once the floor plans were obtained, Olivia confirmed with Michael Wilson that it was still the same layout, and he noted some changes to the inside that were very useful. Olivia then conferred with all the different agencies, explaining their roles, and the timing. At least there were no nearby stores, so the streets could be cleared very quickly.

They were ready to go, and several customers had entered the building, most of them known.

Olivia gave the go ahead, and police cars blocked the surrounding streets. The SWAT team, who had been waiting hidden from sight, then moved in from front and rear, followed by the FBI and the other agencies, snipers on nearby roofs, and police officers going from door to door on neighboring homes telling them to keep low and their doors locked.

It went very well. It was so fast and unexpected that only a couple of shots were fired in warning, and seeing what they were up against, the captors didn't get stupid. A lot of arrests were made, social services came in to oversee the children, and the captors and customers were taken to holding cells to be interviewed. All the children had to be taken to hospital where they were treated in a closed and protected ward.

Special Agent Olivia Danville was very happy with the outcome of the raid, and she ensured that all of the children would be taken care of and given a new start, including Hui and Ning, once they'd been treated and processed.

CHAPTER 20

Another ship was being unloaded, this time in the Port of Boston. On board, there was a shipment of very young girls from Cambodia with no boys, and as the ship docked, they were all put in a container that was specially marked. All the pertinent people had been paid off, so the container would pass through customs with no problems. Once the girls were dressed, made up, and photographed, their pictures would be posted, and then the girls would be sold.

The demand for the children seemed limitless. They all got sold for good prices, and if another ship was to arrive the following day, they would have no problem in selling them either.

The girls would go to all parts of Northern USA. The southern and western states got their own shipments, no state was excluded, and all states had their own perverts who wanted children for sex. If they couldn't have fellow Americans, then they were more than happy to take foreigners who didn't warrant anything like the same attention afforded to the homegrown.

One such regular customer was a man named Stephen Crane who lived in Lincoln, Nebraska. He would always purchase at least three girls, the younger the better, and no matter how many he bought, or how often, no questions were ever asked.

Stephen Crane was a sociopath. Anyone who came across him called him a sick bastard. He'd never been convicted of anything, he had inherited money so didn't work, no one liked him, so they kept on the other side of the street and minded their own business.

Stephen lived in an old farmhouse that was set well back off the road, and its best feature, the main reason he'd bought it apart from its isolation, was the stone cellar. Stephen had a housekeeper once a week, who under no circumstances was allowed into the cellar, and although she was oblivious to what Stephen did down there, she called it the cellar of doom. She couldn't have named it better.

Stephen was a tall man, thin, and his black hair was always swept back with grease. He was as mean looking as he acted. He was always covered in stubble, scars littered his face, and he was just plain ugly. He wasn't dumb though, so he always got his girls from overseas rather than local.

His reputation had come from his schooldays when he would delight in skinning live animals, or decapitating them in front of horrified kids, who were too scared of him to inform the teachers. Sometimes, somebody would be brave enough to take him on, which was always a mistake, as he'd beat them to a pulp. He was in his middle thirties now and about the only folk who would say hello to him were the staff in the stores he frequented, and that was more out of familiarity rather than friendship.

Stephen always picked his girls up just outside Chicago. He knew he could have them delivered to his door, but he just felt safer picking them up far away from his home. It was quite a drive, eight hours each way, and he normally stayed in a motel near to the pickup site, paying cash. The pickup site varied, but it was always remote. He would back up to whatever truck they were using, or they would back up to his, and they would transfer the girls.

Stephen drove a pickup truck and when he picked girls up, he would put a cap on the bed, and throw some blankets inside and plastic bottled water. He would also put in some containers for them to pee in, if needed.

When he went to pick up his new girls that he'd carefully picked from the website, his cellar was newly emptied and thoroughly cleaned. When he'd finished with his girls, one by one, he did the cleanup himself, careful about not making his housekeeper suspicious.

Stephen Crane was in all aspects a serial killer, except he didn't have to look for his victims. As they were illegal, they were never looked for, there were no investigations, and no clues to work with.

He did have two accomplices though, and he really enjoyed watching them having sex with the girls. That was as far as they went, they didn't replicate Stephen's cruelty, but they did condone the killings. In fact, they were grateful that it was he who did that as they didn't think they could do it, but believed it had to happen to preserve their freedom.

One, George Matthews, was the only registered sex offender and had been convicted when he was a soccer coach, for spying on the girls in the shower and for inappropriate touching. The other was one of the cops who had arrested George, and George had noticed the look on his face when he confessed. The cop, Jake Darren, had shown no sign of disgust or horror, he had seem interested if anything at what George had done. When George was released and had returned home to no family, Jake had helped him settle back, found him an apartment, and had given him illegal magazines.

When Stephen had contacted George to ask him if he still liked young girls, and would he like to take advantage of some, George had thought it was a set up so said no. It was only when he realized who Richard was that he thought it wasn't a scam, as not even the police liked Stephen Crane. After George had been allowed to do whatever he wanted to the three girls that Stephen had got from somewhere, he mentioned that he might know someone else who would be interested, and that he would also be able to give them some protection. When George said he was a cop, Stephen insisted on him being unarmed, unwired, and would have to arrive with George, blindfolded. If he didn't have sex with one of the girls, Stephen would take permanent care of him.

The cop thought he was in heaven with three girls to play with. He'd dreamt of it for so long and it had gotten harder for him not to molest his own children or others. He felt bad about it, but that's how he was made.

George and Jake had no idea how Stephen disposed of the girls. They had never asked, and he had never volunteered to tell them. Jake knew the police weren't looking for any young girls, they didn't even know they existed, and until they did, there was nothing to worry about.

Stephen was already in the motel waiting for his shipment to arrive in the morning. This was his most exciting time, taking his delivery and the anticipation of what would happen when he got them home. At this point, the girls would be naive and maybe expecting good things to happen to them, so the look on their faces was more hopeful rather than despair. He thought about their faces as he went to sleep, the ones he'd seen on the website.

After having a good breakfast the following morning, Stephen bought some food from a convenience store and some ice for the water in the truck, and split the rations between his cab and the truck bed. The Cap he had for the bed did have windows, but they were all blacked out, and the only one he left open was the one that faced the back of the truck's cab, which also had a window.

He'd been stopped once, and while the cop checked his plate while sitting in his car, Stephen had waved his gun through the rear window and signaled with his finger on his lips for them to keep quiet and to stay low.

He'd received a speeding ticket, but if the girls had made a noise, or the cop had insisted the rear be opened, he would have shot him and taken his girls elsewhere. He'd already planned for such a scenario, and he was very confident of his plan working if it happened.

Having a little time before the delivery was due, Stephen had another coffee and then relieved himself before returning to his truck and parking it in the designated place. He opened the rear doors and checked the inside again, then casually waited with his back against the truck.

Stephen never knew what his girls would be delivered in, but this time it was a medium sized box truck that were most often used by people moving their own furniture. As Stephen was already in the precise location with his rear doors already opened, the moving truck backed right up to them, only stopping for a moment for the front passenger to open the rear doors and to get into the back, before the driver reversed some more.

The driver left his engine running as he came around to Stephen, and after checking Stephen's I.D., showed him the three pictures of the girls, asking if they were the right ones.

Stephen said yes, and the driver yelled out the numbers to his friend who moved the three girls to the back. There was still enough space for Stephen to see, and he nodded to the driver as the three girls got into the back of his truck. The driver handed the pictures to Stephen, and then returned to his truck to move it forward a few feet. His friend jumped out of the back and locked the doors, as Stephen did the same with his. Stephen watched them drive away, wondering where they were taking the other girls he'd glimpsed, then got into his cab and drove in the opposite direction toward home. He hadn't asked the driver, but when he bought the girls he stipulated that he didn't want them touched. If the drivers had raped them, as they were sometimes allowed to do, then he would have got his money returned and three free girls. The drivers knew the rules, and so far Stephen had never had recourse to make a complaint. A broken rule had fatal results.

The ride home went without incidence, and on arriving, Stephen opened the front door and then the cellar door before letting the girls out. There was another door to the cellar from the outside, but Stephen didn't want them to know about it, and it was heavily disguised on the inside.

At gun point, he quickly ushered them through the house and down the steps to the cellar, and they stood together scared and silently in the middle of the room. One side contained three made up cots and a sitting area, and the other side had a washing machine and dryer, a refrigerator, larder, microwave, and an ominous looking cage with a stained table, straps, and a couple of locked cabinets.

There was also a large open closet on the bed side of the room, with an enclosed bathroom next to it. The closet was full of clothing sorted in different sizes and the bathroom afforded some privacy. Except that Stephen had cameras set up everywhere, mostly hidden, so there was no privacy at all.

Having pointed everything out, Stephen left the three very cute girls in his cellar, as he went back outside and checked the bed of the truck.

One of the three disposable toilets had been used and he threw that away along with the used water bottles and eaten food. What they hadn't used he saved for the next trip, except for the food.

After locking up his truck, he went inside, made himself something to eat, got a beer from the fridge, then watched the television for a while. The live feed from the secure cellar.

Stephen wouldn't tell his two accomplices about the new girls until he'd taken their virginities. Then he would watch the two men with the girls, as a voyeur, and start to have his fun inside the cage.

The only time the girls would get a break would be on the housekeeper's day. There was another washer and dryer in the kitchen for Stephen's laundry, and he would pretend to be working in the cellar with music on when she came, making sure the girls stayed quiet. It was a routine and it worked.

CHAPTER 21

Special Agent John Wells was working undercover in Washington D.C. The FBI had by now become suspicious of the goings on at Justin and Troy Reynolds house, and wanted to know what was going on in there.

Several weeks prior, a male prostitute had been arrested by the police, no big deal, but his lawyer had asked to speak to the FBI. Purely out of courtesy and curiosity, an agent was dispatched to go and talk to the guy and his lawyer. It seemed the prostitute had a tale to tell, so he was brought to the FBI offices.

His story was that he used to work for Justin and Troy, they had bought him when he was twelve years old, after he had been taken from his home in the Philippines. He was drugged by them, and was then forced into having sex with very many men, after Justin and Troy had first raped him. After a while, he got used to the sex and as he was looked after, he no longer cared. When Justin and Troy eventually told him that his services were being less and less asked for, as their clients preferred the younger boys, they told him that he was welcome to stay at the house and oversee the boys in a supervisory role. He would be paid for doing this, but could also find his own clients away from the house if he wished, and any money he earned would be his own. He could also leave the house permanently if he preferred.

However, there was one condition. If he ever mentioned that he worked for Justin and Troy, to the police, not only would it never get to court or even be reported, his life, and whoever else was in it, would also be over. This condition had been acceptable, and he carried on working for the two men until he met someone and moved in with him.

Everything had been going fine until he arrived home one day to find his partner had been beaten to death in their home, and a message written in his blood saying "We told you not to talk." He couldn't understand it, but instead of reporting it, he went and got drunk, was arrested, and then asked to speak to the FBI.

After going through the correct channels, the FBI thought the story was bogus, the police had no record of anyone being killed, and there was no sign of anything suspicious at the man's apartment. So the FBI sent him back to the police, who released him with a caution, and that was the end of the story.

That is until he turned up dead a couple of weeks later. The police ruled it as suicide with a self-inflicted gunshot to the head. The problem for the FBI was that the gunshot was to the right side of the head, yet he was left handed.

So the FBI set up a discreet surveillance of Justin and Troy's house. They were astounded at who they pictured entering, and when they looked at Justin's and Troy's finances, and the junk they sold, they sent for Special Agent John Wells.

Working undercover in D.C. held no danger to John Wells, nobody knew him in town, and pretending to be gay was no problem for him. Justin and Troy were openly gay, so it made complete sense to send in an agent who was also gay. He was by no means the only gay in the FBI, but undercover he was the best, if what they suspected was actually going on in the Reynolds home.

Putting the names to the faces in the photographs was easy, and John set to work ingratiating himself with some of them. It was difficult work, you had to do it slowly and gradually to gain trust and become a familiar face.

John Wells knew no-one in D.C. apart from a few agents he had trained with at Quantico. Unlike a lot of his peers who loved D.C. and the prestige of working in the nation's capital, John didn't like it at all. It was too political for him, and as soon as his work was done, they would hopefully send him back to the Pacific Northwest.

John was the classic, "He's too good looking to be straight," guy. He himself didn't think of himself that way, but he was tall, well dressed, thick wavy black hair, blue eyes, and all the hours he spent in the gym or swimming, made him lean and strong. He took care of his skin as well, with lots of different creams and moisturizers. It made him smell clean, fresh, but very unmanly, although the attention he received from the female agents was the envy of the rest of the males.

Under the alias of 'Simon Walker', John was pretending to be an interior designer who'd been brought to D.C. by his client who was moving from

Connecticut. To enforce his new profession, James had business cards and magazine clippings of his work, along with a website if anyone were to check up on him. John had worked extensively for several years setting up aliases, and he kept the websites and Facebook pages updated to keep them looking fresh.

Simon Walker had already become friendly with some of the Reynolds friends, and had even met Justin and Troy themselves. Simon had made it known, very discreetly, that he preferred younger boys for his sexual pleasure, but he didn't push with his new friends, knowing that patience was the key element. So he kept going to the right places, eating or drinking alone until someone joined him, or asked him to join them as he worked on his laptop or iPad.

Simon's method paid off and he eventually got his invite.

A team was set up and it was left to 'Simon' to give the signal. No one knew if security measures were taken inside the house, or even for certain if anything untoward was going on. Although they had a warrant, they would still look very foolish if they invaded and found nothing, so it was down to 'Simon'. His phone had been cloned, so they would hear everything that went on, but if the phone was taken off him they'd be in the dark. They also didn't want to wire 'Simon', as then he could be found out before they got anywhere.

Simon went in alone, taken by his new 'friend' Anthony, who was a high end civil lawyer with a top firm in D.C. There was no security, no frisking, or even any questions asked, and at first Simon thought it was all a bust as it just seemed like a cocktail party for men only. Young men handed out drinks and appetizers, the talk was light and entertaining, and the hosts were welcoming and jovial.

After almost an hour of this, Simon was sitting down with Anthony who spoke quietly into his ear.

"In a moment, some boys will appear and they will be holding different items with different prices. You buy the item and it comes with the boy, and then the boy will take you to his room after either Justin or Troy takes your credit card for the sale. If there is more than one interest in a boy, there will be a short auction. Are you ready?"

"I'm ready and very excited Anthony, thank you for bringing me along."

"A pleasure Simon, you're going to have fun."

Just as Anthony said, several boys came into the room carrying different items with varying prices, and the boys stood in a line, quietly and without expression.

Once Justin and Troy finished their conversations, they brought the room's attention to them by clapping their hands.

"Our little sale can now commence friends," announced Justin. "As you can see, these are bargain prices, guaranteed to give you immense pleasure, if only for a few seconds," he smiled, gaining a few laughs from around the room.

Simon had been looking at the boys and they were all minors. The youngest was the most expensive and he guessed the cheapest was the oldest. Most of the boys he guessed, were from the Philippines, with a couple from Mexico.

"We'll start with our most expensive product this evening," continued Justin standing behind the first boy. "This is Matthew and he's a very agile boy. So which among you thinks you can handle our little Matthew?"

Simon raised his arm.

"'Ooh, our new friend Simon is obviously a man with taste. If anyone else has an interest in Matthew, it isn't too late. Simon is getting a bargain for this vase he's getting, it's an absolute steal. Any other buyers?"

Justin looked around hopefully, but this time there would be no auction. He thought he would do better with the next boy.

"Then the vase is yours Simon, look after it, and Troy will take your payment."

As Simon handed over the credit card to Troy who swiped it on a small device attached to his phone, the next sale was already underway, this time for a boy named Gerald. Simon signed the phone, he was handed the vase, and the boy Matthew took his hand and led him away. Gerald was being auctioned between three of the men.

Simon, in his interior designer mode, had admired the furnishings and decor within the home as it was all of the same Georgian period. It had been put together very expertly and expensively, and he'd told the hosts so.

As Matthew led the way, 'Simon' kept his eyes open and observant as he admired more of the furnishings. Cameras were discreetly hidden in various places, and there were more in Matthew's room, which interestingly had a lock on the outside.

On entering the room, Matthew closed it behind them and then posed seductively on the large bed. In his broken English, Matthew asked Simon to undress him and then himself, but Simon said he needed to wash up first, and went into the doorless bathroom. Knowing he was being filmed, Simon took a pee as he pulled out his cellphone, and looked at a text, which he replied to before shaking himself and going to the washbasin to wash his hands. Looking around, he saw Matthew waiting for him, totally naked now and leaning on the open doorway, stroking himself.

Simon was hearing a ruckus from below and knew what was happening, so he ran to Matthew and pushed him toward the bed, telling him to get his clothes on. Matthew had no idea what this man was doing, but he did as he was told, thinking it was just another game, putting on his clothing again as the man casually sat down.

As Matthew buttoned up his shirt, armed men dressed in black and wearing helmets burst into the room, and told the two to get down on the floor and put their arms behind their backs, at which point their wrists were tied with plastic ties and they were instructed not to move. The armed men moved on and they heard shouts and protests, warnings made, as the task force swept through the house.

Within minutes, Simon and Matthew were hauled back to their feet and marched out, along with everybody else who had been in the house. Some of the inhabitants were still protesting, threatening jobs and livelihoods as everyone was escorted outside to the waiting vehicles. Simon was treated like everyone else and put into a prisoner transport vehicle, being told by some of the other customers not to say anything and ask for a lawyer.

On arriving at the FBI building, they were met by the flashing light bulbs of the media, so nearly everyone ducked their head as much as possible, outraged at being photographed and filmed.

Although they had already been read their rights at the scene, they were done so again as fingerprints were taken, mug shots done, and then taken one by one to interview rooms from the holding cells.

Simon had learned a couple of things from being transported and from the cells, which he gladly passed on to the task force. After he was taken back to the cells, a short while later he was told he was being released as his bail had been met, and he returned to being John Wells.

The bust was a huge success. Everybody was shocked at the names that were arrested, and house searches unearthed more evidence against the defendants. A lot of the boys were very uncooperative with law enforcement, but that was normal. Almost everyone else wanted to make a deal of some sort, to lessen their pain and humiliation.

The boy Matthew was able to disclose his real name and from where he'd come, along with a couple of other names. One of the names, Bec, tied in with an arrest that had been made in New Jersey, and from what they learned from Justin and Troy's computers, they soon had a handle on the operation that had brought the kids over from the Philippines.

As the boys went to Victim Services to start the long process of convincing them that they were the victims and to reclaim their former lives, the adults were looking at long prison sentences even after plea bargaining. They would also lose their families, who had been publicly shamed by their actions, which to some of them was by far the worst punishment.

The FBI were overjoyed at this success, and those involved had a celebratory night before returning to their desks the following day. To follow up on the leads and to start fresh investigations against the relentless tide of child abuse.

CHAPTER 22

Ashley was now unrecognizable from the innocent and pretty twelve year old girl that she had once been. She was fifteen now and the drugs and the atrocious treatment of her body had taken its toll.

Her pimp didn't care if she ate, he just wanted the cash she earned from lying on her back, and he didn't care about Ashley making her arms look like pin cushions. It was actually better for business that her drug taking and lack of protein was keeping her body from fully developing, as it kept her looking young.

But now it had gone too far. She was getting gaunt, shadows had formed around her eyes, her teeth were rotting and yellow from smoking between hits, so she wasn't as popular as she'd once been. So the pimp put her on the street with the older women. It was different rules on the streets. Ashley had to find her own customers, and if she didn't, she was beaten around the ribs and didn't get her fix.

Some of the women tried to help her with advice, to try and keep looking as pretty as she could so that Johns would stop and talk to her. But the women were in the same boat as she, and they also had to get customers and cash.

By now, Ashley really was in another world. She had no memories at all of her former life and family, her only schooling in recent years was how to treat her customers and satisfy their needs. Ashley's only need was her drugs.

Despite the physical state she was in, her pimp had her dress like a naughty schoolgirl, with a tiny pleated skirt, a blouse unbuttoned almost to her waist, and ripped stockings held up by a garter belt. The black heels made her legs look even thinner than they were, and make up was plastered heavily to her face.

Seeing a car moving slowly toward her and the driver giving her a look, Ashley sashayed her way to the curb, and to the open window on the passenger side. Just as she was about to poke her head through the opening, a woman down the line shouted a warning. "He's a cop!"

Taking the warning seriously, Ashley still poked her head through the open window and said, "Hey, are you looking for directions or something?"

By now Ashley spoke all the time in the soft voice she'd been taught to use in the hotel.

Knowing his cover was now blown, the vice cop asked Ashley how old she was.

Ashley truly had no idea how old she was, but her pimp had told her to always say nineteen if she was ever asked by a cop, so that's what she did.

"You sure kid?" He asked. "Let me see your driving license."

"I ain't got it with me, and I wasn't planning on driving anywhere. I don't have no time for any chit chat, so I'm going now. You have a good day sir."

"Okay kid, I'm not going to keep you, but I haven't seen you around here before. Is there anything I can do for you?" He asked nicely.

"I'll take a cigarette if you have one."

He handed her a cigarette and a Bic lighter to fire it up, and she dropped the lighter on the passenger seat as she took a puff, walking away with a little wave.

As the detective drove off, he saw her in his rear view mirror talking to a john who had pulled up behind him, and wondered how much she was asking of him for whatever services he was wanting.

As the cop turned onto another street, he didn't see her climbing into the john's car.

Back at the police station, the cop had been unable to shake the image of the girl out of his head, and as he parked, he looked at the lighter still on the passenger seat.

Like a lot of cops, he carried little evidence bags around, so he very carefully picked up the lighter with a clean tissue and put it in a bag. Once inside the building, he stopped by forensics and asked them to run any prints they could get from the lighter, whenever they had chance.

It was actually a few days before he got the result. He'd almost forgotten about it, but as soon as he was handed the piece of paper, he was calling the FBI.

Special Agent Olivia Danville heard about it a few minutes later as it had been her case. Although she was very busy with suspected trafficking houses in Sacramento, San Francisco and San Jose, she remembered Ashley and Sandy and was glad that at least one of them had shown up, and alive.

She wanted though to be sure that it was a definite I.D. She didn't want to give false hope to the family who by now probably thought their daughter was dead. She was dismayed to discover that Ashley was still out there working the streets, which was another reason not to inform the family just yet.

The FBI agent who had called her was just as frustrated, but when he explained the circumstances and that the detective, along with another agent was right now trying to locate her, Olivia calmed down. They'd waited this long, a little more time wouldn't hurt, and she could well imagine what state the girl was in. The detective had actually done a heads up job and should be commended.

Two hours later, Ashley was dropped off by a john in his car at the same point the detective had spoken to her, days earlier, and where he and the agent were waiting. She was still dressed the same way, but she didn't want to go with him or the agent to the station. They eventually bundled her into the back of the car as she cursed like a seasoned trooper, and they had a squad car pick up her recent john.

Ashley was very hostile. She didn't understand what was happening and if she wasn't under arrest, then she should be released immediately, or have a phone call so that she could be picked up. Instead, she was medically inspected, swabs were taken, and a social worker was trying to talk to her, telling her a whole bunch of lies.

The vice cop knew which pimp ran that particular part of town and he picked him up and deposited him with the FBI. Although they were unable to arrest him, mainly because of Ashley's refusal to acknowledge who he was, they were able to really scare him by informing him that once Ashley recovered her senses, then he would probably be arrested for rape of a minor, keeping her against her will, administering and supplying class A drugs to her, and for soliciting her. Which would mean a very lengthy prison sentence, along with a lifetime of being a registered sex offender.

Once Ashley's identity was confirmed, Olivia managed to convince the Las Vegas office to transfer her to San Francisco, as it would help in her recovery for her family to be around. Ashley was now taking Naloxone which was the only antidote to heroin, but she was going to have to undergo many weeks of therapy to even get close to knowing who she actually was, and she would have to be kept in a contained environment, otherwise she would run.

Olivia visited Ashley's family to tell them she'd been found, but to warn them of what to expect. Although it was good news she was telling them, there was a lot of bad stuff that the doctors had discovered, which was heartbreaking to reveal and to take in.

What the family really needed to understand was that Ashley would reject them at first, would be abusive, and that a lot of patience was needed with her. Eventually, she would recover, many others before her had, but it took time.

Olivia had the whole family crying as she explained what Ashley had no doubt gone through, from the very first moment of being taken. From experience in dealing with victims, she knew it was better for the family to know details so they could deal with it as soon as possible. She'd known cases where the families had asked questions after their child had almost recovered, and it had always resulted in a setback in their recovery. It can be very difficult to understand that even children can be helpless in what happens to them, that they can't fight back when something really bad is happening to them.

CHAPTER 23

Janelle was a twelve year old girl living in Boston, Mass. She was the daughter of an unmarried mother who was a junkie, and Janelle had been taken away from her Mom because her Mom wouldn't, or couldn't, get off the drugs.

Ever since she'd been a baby, Janelle's Mom had turned tricks to feed her addiction and her baby, but as Janelle had gotten older, the men that Mom brought home had turned their attention to her, and that was when social services stepped in.

Janelle really missed her Mom, but she knew she needed help, and the apartment they had lived in was dirty, infested with cockroaches, and the neighborhood dangerous. Whoever Janelle's father was, her Mom had no idea, and no one had ever come forward to suggest it may have been them. Mom had also never talked about relatives or ever visited anyone.

So Janelle had been taken away and for the past three years had been in a foster home, with her own bedroom, regular meals, and school. She also had a foster father that wouldn't leave her alone.

Janelle was a pretty girl of African descent, tall for her age, already developing into a young woman, brown eyed, and she kept her hair short and straightened. She got away with saying she was sixteen, but in reality her childhood had been lost, as she'd had to grow up much faster than girls of the same age.

Several weeks previous, she had met a young man named Michael in a Starbucks, when he asked her if she minded him sitting at her table in the crowded coffee bar. Michael was a sharp looking guy, said he was twenty two, dressed well in chinos and a polo shirt, and was very quiet as he worked on his laptop and sipped his latte. It was Janelle who engaged him in conversation, asking him if his drink was good and what he did for a living.

Michael said he was a dealer of various imported goods, and he treated her like the sixteen year old schoolgirl that she said she was. Since that original meeting, he had taken her to the movies a couple of times, to dinner and lunch, walks around the harbor, and shopping in the mall. Janelle regarded Michael as her boyfriend, and although she hadn't slept with him at that point, she had let him touch her and had reciprocated. She had really liked kissing him.

Unbeknown to Janelle, Michael was very aware that she wasn't sixteen. He'd seen the discrepancy on her Facebook page and although she had changed her status to having a boyfriend called Michael, he'd kept her from taking a photo of him, and Michael wasn't even his real name. He'd looked her up almost as soon as she gave him her name in Starbucks, knew she was an unhappy foster child, and perfect for what he had planned for her. When he described himself as an importer of various goods, it was normally young girls from Mexico, the Far East, or Africa. He had to pay for those, so when he got an opportunity to groom a home grown girl for free, he took it, especially one from an ethnic minority. If they happened to be orphans or fostered, it was even better, as there was rarely a search done for them.

A couple of weeks after meeting, Michael had taken Janelle to a motel, not a rundown place, it appeared very respectable, and the interior of the rooms were very nice. Clean, well furnished, air conditioned, and very comfortable. Michael had taken her virginity there, with no protests from Janelle, as she believed she was in love and that's what lovers did.

The following morning, Michael had played around with her, showing her various things that he said he liked and Janelle had only been too willing to oblige. Then he told her what he expected from her, as he was in economic trouble and he needed her to help him out for a while.

Every so often a man would come to the room and he would expect to be taken care of, the way that Michael had shown her. The room would be her home now. He would take her to buy a new wardrobe, there'd be no more school, and she could eat at the diner across the street. The room would be cleaned every day when she went for breakfast, but it was her responsibility to make the bed during the day and to keep the room looking nice until the morning clean. This wouldn't last for long. It was just until he repaid some money he owed, but if she tried to run away then both of them would be tortured and then killed. Michael was sorry, but he'd fallen in love with her and would repay her for what she did to help him out. Hearing the word love had Janelle agreeing with him, and two hours later a man came in to her room, followed by another one after he left, and yet another one after him.

Michael did take her shopping, and sometimes he would stay the night using a condom, although most of the men didn't, saying they hated to use them. Michael had obtained birth pills and told Janelle to use them, to be safe, and whenever he stayed he always told her how much he loved her.

Michael had three other girls in the motel, and he treated them the same way, telling them how much he loved them, and that one day soon they would be able to go south and find a beach to live by, and be partners for life.

CHAPTER 24

The FBI office in Dallas had its own Violent Crimes Against Children Section, and it too was always busy. There were plenty of gangs on the other side of the border with Mexico who were only too willing to smuggle and sell their compatriots children. Very often the kids had a dual purpose. To be mules for the drugs and then sold to the highest bidder. If they didn't do as they were told, the gangs were ruthless. All the kids were fully aware that their families would be slaughtered if they tried to run away, and probably put on public display to deter any other kids from fleeing.

It was one thing knowing that children were being trafficked, but it was quite another to find them before they got older. It didn't matter to the FBI or to the police if the children were being used for sex, labor or both. They wanted to find them, and especially the folks who had bought them or sold them.

Special Agent Dusty Johnson knew there were at least a couple of houses in the Dallas area alone that were soliciting young children for sex. Mainly girls, but boys as well. He knew about them because an informant of his, a pimp with questionable morals, had told him so as they were taking away some of his business. The pimp had no problem whatsoever with adults being used for sex, but as a father he couldn't tolerate children being exploited and turned into brainless drug addicts.

Dusty, who was no relation to the golfer of the same name but heard about it every time he teed up, was a veteran now, but the job never got any easier. The only part about it he loved was when they got the convictions, and the perpetrators were sent to prison for a very long time, and would have to face the wrath of the other inmates. He didn't take them to prison himself, but he really wished he could, if only to see their petrified faces as they entered the gates.

It was difficult now for Dusty to keep in shape. Seemed like everything he ate or drank, which wasn't much, stuck to his waistline and even his daily morning jog didn't help. He got sympathy from his wife who was having her own battle, but not from his grown kids and colleagues. Apart from his weight, Dusty was balding, so he shaved his whole head every morning which to his pleasure, made people think he was not to be messed with. Which was very amusing to his long standing wife. Another reason he shaved his head smooth, was that he was grey now, totally, so he looked a little younger and meaner until he put his reading glasses on.

With a little help from the pimp, he had an undercover agent looking for underage sex, and the pimp had let it be known in the right circles. The undercover agent was just waiting for a call, as he already knew that someone had been checking his fake background.

The latest batch of trafficked children, like all the other kids, had been dressed up and the girls had make up applied for their photos, before being sold.

As was fairly usual, the website and the code to enter the auction was well protected, and it was extremely difficult to get a new customer on their list, which the agent was hoping for, or at least to be invited to one of the houses as a paying customer.

Dusty was also still getting a lot of pressure from the local politicians about the rich girl from Highland Park who had now been missing for months. He and his team, along with the local police, had spent hundreds of man hours looking for her but it was a dead end. No clues whatsoever had turned up, just gossip, and they'd even investigated those like weird teachers, jealous school friends, odd neighbors, or strangers in particular places. All the registered sex offenders had been questioned and their properties searched, but nothing had materialized. That didn't seem to matter to the politicians and the press. They wanted the girl found and complained at the supposed inactivity of the law enforcement, who in their opinion, should be out on the streets looking for her every minute of the day.

The man who had her, Richard Brand, was getting a little bored with her now since all the initial excitement. Some days he just made sure she was fed and left her alone. He'd never used her real name. He'd read somewhere that a captive should engage in personal chatter so that they would be liked, and therefore less likely to be killed. So Richard had avoided getting to know her. He didn't think he would kill her, but he didn't want to like her. He hadn't taken her for her mind, it was purely for her young body.

Retrieving his mail one day from the box at the
end of his driveway, he was surprised to find an extra
envelope concealed within a grocery store's coupons.
Inside, were half a dozen pictures of young girls, fees
for certain amounts of time, and a phone number to
call if he was interested. If he called the number, he
would only be permitted two minutes to ask
questions.

Richard didn't have much money, he survived on
government handouts, but he did save cash when he
could, and he was also thinking of selling the house
but still living in it until he died. The idea was more
and more appealing to Richard the more he thought
about it, and he smiled thinking of the new tenants
finding his secret cellar.

After taking care of his rich girl as he called her,
feeding her and having sex with her limp body,
Richard drove to the nearby convenience store.
There, he called the number from the public phone.

"Hello," a man replied.

"Is this a trap?" Richard asked. "Are you trying to
get me arrested? How did you find me?"

"All sex offenders addresses are public knowledge
sir. If you get arrested then so do we and we don't
want that to happen. Tell me if you are interested in
any of the photos we sent you before I hang up." The
man was matter of fact and emotionless.

"Yes I am," Richard admitted, worrying if the call
was being recorded and he asked directly if he was.

"No, you are not being recorded. Call me back
tomorrow at around the same time and tell me which
photo interests you. Then you can tell me your name

and how you wish to pay, although cash is the safest option."

"How do you know I'm not a cop?"

"Right now I don't. But I will once you give me your name and I make some checks. Time is up sir, call me tomorrow." The man hung up before Richard could ask more questions.

Richard was excited again but also worried. He didn't want to go back to prison, he felt he should never have been there in the first place, but he did have this weakness in his psyche.

He called back the following day and ordered a very young looking girl, for sure she was younger than the rich girl, and he said he would pay cash. Giving his name, the man at the other end of the line asked Richard who his last cell mate was in prison. Richard gave the name, and was then asked when he wanted the girl, and for how long.

Richard suggested the following afternoon, but on being told that was too soon and that the girl wouldn't be available until the following week, as she was in high demand, Richard agreed and made the appointment. He was to make his way to a bookstore on Preston Road and wait in the coffee bar, then he would be taken to the girl from there.

Returning home, Richard had the image of the small Mexican girl he was going to hook up with ingrained in his mind, as he went down the steps to his rich girl.

As was almost normal, the rich girl was watching television from the only chair, dressed simply in leggings and a tee shirt. Richard had bought her few clothes apart from the initial ones. It was too dangerous for him, but he had ventured into a Goodwill store once, and seeing no cameras had purchased some clothing.

Knowing what was expected of her, she began to disrobe as he came through the door and Richard did so as well. Within a few minutes, Richard was getting dressed again, and as he checked her supplies, she spoke from her prone position on the bed.

"I think I'm pregnant," she said in her soft voice.

Richard looked around, shock on his face.

"What the hell do you mean? You don't look pregnant," he defiantly stated, staring at her flat stomach.

"You knew my periods had started, but you've never worn any protection. I missed my last period and I'm late again. I think I'm pregnant."

She'd put her hands on her stomach and Richard remembered her bleeding, buying her some tampons and pads from a pharmacy three counties away.

"So you think you're pregnant because you missed your last period. That's just great, why didn't you say something sooner?" Richard asked, his annoyance obvious in the tone of his voice.

"I don't know, but my tits are sensitive as well. I think you should get me a test kit."

Richard couldn't believe it, and he was pissed that he'd have to take a lengthy drive just to get her a kit to pee on. He wondered what he would do if the test was positive. Without saying anything else, he stormed out of the cellar to take a drive, as he wanted to know now if she was or not. He couldn't stop cursing to himself as he drove away, and he was still swearing two hours later when he returned.

Going back downstairs and finding her back in the chair, in the same leggings and shirt as before and watching television again, he threw the test kit at her and told her to go and pee on it. Watching her as she did so, as there was no privacy on the toilet.

Sitting on the chair she'd vacated, he waited, worrying, until she put the test result in front of his face. She didn't say anything, she didn't have to, the result was positive.

Over the next few days, Richard delighted in hurting the rich girl's tender breasts, her winces being more enjoyable to him than her usual no emotion. He also decided that he would have to kill her, there was just no way he could have a baby in the house. He had no idea how he would do it, or even if he had the courage.

Doing as he'd been told, Richard was in the bookstore at the designated time, and he was drinking a cappuccino when a strange man sat down opposite him. He looked fierce and very dangerous to Richard, like many of the prisoners he'd encountered in prison.

"Are you ready Richard?" He growled in a low voice.

"How do you know my name is Richard?"

"We're not stupid. Have you never heard of pictures?" He asked with obvious contempt in his voice, and showed Richard his own photo on the cell phone he was holding.

The picture was of Richard leaving his house just minutes ago.

"Time is money Richard, and you are wasting yours. Follow mc out, not too close, and I'll take you for a ride."

The man, who had never identified himself, got up and he was bigger than Richard had thought, but he followed him out and across the street to the parking lot. He had a black Lincoln SUV and he motioned to Richard to get into the rear seat of the tinted vehicle. The big man got in on the other side, and they started moving straight away.

"Are you the man on the phone?" Richard asked.

"No. You will never meet him. Now open your shirt so I can see you're not wired."

"Me? Wired? Are you kidding me?"

"Open your shirt Mr., this is compulsory, as is a frisk down. Soon as we get it done, you put the mask on and we get to your little girl. So open your shirt," he ordered.

Richard did so, felt the man's large hands frisk him, and then the darkness as the mask, or sack, was put over his head.

Until the engine was turned off by the unknown driver, Richard stayed quiet and only spoke when he was asked for the money, telling the big man it was in his left jacket pocket. He felt him taking the money out, and heard the notes rustle as they were counted.

"We're at the destination, but don't try to take off your mask. We'll take it off once we're inside, and we'll put it back on you when we take you back. Now take off your seatbelt, and we'll take you inside."

Richard unhooked the belt, and then he was manhandled out of the car and walked a few steps before he was able to see again. He thought he was in a house of some sort, very nicely furnished, and another strange man was standing before him, another burly character who had a gun in a holster on his right hip. He told Richard the rules.

"I'm going to take you upstairs in a moment to your girl. You have paid for two hours with her. When that time is over, I will come into the room and bring you back down here, whether you have finished with her or not. The room is soundproof so make as much noise as you want, but if you hit the girl or strangle her, anything other than slapping her ass, you will not leave this place alive. You are welcome to any of the drinks in the fridge, but don't give the girl alcohol. She has no name so you can call her what you want, and she will do anything you want her to. Her English isn't very good but if you signal to her what you want she will do it. If she doesn't, tell us, and we will administer her punishment and give you a free appointment. Do you understand Richard?"

"Yes."

"Then follow me. Your two hours start now."

The man consulted his watch and led the way upstairs, stopping along the landing at a door and unlocking it, like it was a hotel room. Only difference was that you couldn't open the door from the inside.

He gently pushed Richard inside, told him not to forget the rules, and closed the door on him.

Unbeknown to Richard, the undercover agent from Special Agent Johnson's squad had obtained an invite, paid his money, and an hour into Richard's allotted two hours the house was being raided on all sides by various law enforcement agencies. It was two cops who actually broke down the door on Richard's room, and they found him in a very compromising position with the minor, which tested their emotional control to the utmost. It's one thing to be warned what to expect, but to see it with your own eyes is something else entirely. The only thing that prevented the cops from taking the law into their own hands, was knowing that if they did so the guy would walk away, and it could well be themselves who served time. So they did what they'd been told to do by the FBI, making sure they made no mistakes as they read Richard his rights, arrested him, passed the girl to social services, and secured the room until it could be processed. Then they made their reports.

Richard was devastated. Being handcuffed and marched passed disgusted faces, he faced the reality of going back to prison for the rest of his life, unless he could make a deal. He demanded a lawyer.

Special Agent Johnson was puzzled by Richard's lawyer wanting a deal. Richard, as far as the Special Agent was aware, was only a customer. He didn't have anything to deal with and hadn't even been on the radar before the raid, yet here was his lawyer demanding a deal for a vastly reduced sentence. It didn't make any sense, but each day the lawyer would be calling, not giving any details, but saying that if a deal could be made, then a major case would be closed.

The lack of information was annoying, so the special agent got a warrant and searched Richard's house again. They found nothing, and the neighbors, although they didn't like Richard, had nothing to share. Almost at a dead end, the special agent called in a cadaver dog, thinking maybe a body was buried somewhere.

The dog sniffed around outside, front and back, all to no avail, so the special agent brought him and his handler inside. The dog was trained to smell dead bodies beneath the earth, but when the handler came to the special agent saying the dog was acting strange, but hadn't found a dead body, it was curious. The dog was scratching in a closet, whimpering, but not barking, as if he had smelled a cat or something. So he had the dog taken away, and had a couple of agents look around in the empty closet, who thought their boss was going crazy. Until they found the latch that raised the carpet and revealed the steps.

The special agent followed his men down the steps with guns drawn, and they were aghast when they found the girl. Here, after all the months looking for her, and the house had previously been searched many times. If Richard Brand or his lawyer had mentioned which major case they were trying to deal with sooner, the special agent knew he would have made the deal. He would have been forced to do so. Richard Brand would have served time, but not much. Now, he would never experience freedom ever again.

On hearing that there was going to be no deal, and that he was also facing charges of kidnapping, rape of a minor and a host of other charges, Richard almost came to blows with his lawyer.

One irony that came out of finding the pregnant girl, was that her father, who was a vociferous proponent of pro-life whatever the circumstances, suddenly changed his tune. Whether it was because of family pressure, or because it was his own daughter, he allowed her to undergo an abortion, and never again campaigned for pro-life.

Closing down that operation in the house was very satisfying to Special Agent Johnson, but there was a lot more to do. One case ended, another one opened.

CHAPTER 25

The pimp in Vegas had been picked up again and arrested, once Ashley's identity and medical tests had been confirmed. The really bad news for him was that he hadn't been as strict with her cleanliness as they had in the hotel, and they had found his DNA along with the arrested john's inside Ashley. He knew the charges would only get worse once the girl's mind began to recover, so he instructed his attorney to negotiate a deal as soon as possible, and get immunity from any future charges. In return, he would give them the address and the names of the people he dealt with in Las Vegas, who had a great number of children under their control. If he had to serve a short amount of time then fine, except not to be in a prison amongst the trafficker's people, which were a very well known gang.

So the attorney went to work, back and forth, trying to get his client the best deal possible. Eventually, the deal was made, the pimp would serve a short amount of time in a Federal low security penitentiary, and he gave the address and name of the hotel, along with the names of the people he'd dealt with.

Putting the hotel under surveillance while the Task Force was put together, it became obvious that it was going to be one of the biggest busts due to the size of the hotel, and the number of customers it was getting. It was a very neat operation, and just by taking in regular hotel guests, it avoided any suspicions.

On the day of the raid, everybody who left the hotel before the designated hour was picked up a few blocks away and had their phones confiscated. As they had done in Los Angeles, the surrounding streets were blocked off as soon as they moved in. A lot of gunfire was heard as law enforcement swept through, and in the command truck they had a lot of requests for "Man down," along with a lot of yelling and threats. It was a very worrying time, and seemed to go on for an eternity, with pockets of resistance who seemed determined not to be captured.

Of course, it wasn't very long into the raid that the media showed up, and even from their safe gathering point, the microphones picked up the sounds of the gunfire, and the reporters were trying to describe what was going on even though they had yet to be told. Most of them were guessing that it was a drug bust, as DEA agents had been seen along with all the other agencies. The cops who were keeping them behind the tapes were saying nothing, apart from mentioning there would be a press conference as soon as possible. Even the news channel helicopters were kept at a safe distance, but it didn't prevent them filming the top of the hotel from quite a distance away.

Once the ambulances started moving in and then leaving shortly after with sirens blaring, it was clear that whatever had gone on in the hotel was now over, and soon forensic teams were arriving along with social services. The media were then told there would be a short press conference within minutes, where they were waiting, and the crews set up their microphones together until there were almost a dozen of them waiting for someone to speak into them.

When five people in suits approached, three men and two women, the media pressed forward and cell phones were hoisted into the air as one of the women took the stand.

"Good afternoon, and thank you for your patience," she spoke with authority and clarity. "I am Special Agent in Charge Wilson, and today, with much help from fellow law enforcement agencies, we conducted a joint raid on the Hotel Oasis, which we believe was operating as a Child Prostitution Ring. Our suspicions were correct. We think that most of the children that we have taken into care, were trafficked into the USA, but there are also children that are home grown. It will take time to determine all the facts, as a lot of the children's English is not very good. Apart from being prostituted, we are accumulating evidence that they were also drugged, beaten, and tortured. We are still processing the crime scene and it will take some time, but we were able to witness some of the goings on when we entered and searched the various rooms. As of this moment, we have forty three minors receiving treatment, mostly girls, but several boys as well." She paused for a moment, looking at the reporters, who looked shocked and disbelieving, before continuing.

"After receiving a very reliable tip off, we put the hotel under surveillance while we got together a team and a search warrant. While we were watching, we recognized many convicted sex offenders entering and leaving the hotel, along with members of a certain gang, who we know have long running ties to human trafficking, child prostitution, and drug dealing. As you may have heard, we encountered a lot of resistance inside the hotel, and there have been fatalities from both sides. I cannot give details yet on who, or how many, as families need to be informed and we still have people in surgery. But I do want to make it clear that these very brave law enforcement personnel knew exactly what they were going into, and with no hesitation they all wanted to do so. I knew some of them personally, and I am extremely proud that I did so. This is a ruthless gang we were dealing with, we all knew it, and they would rather die than spend the rest of their years in prison. All bar one gang member was killed, and the one who survived is now under heavy guard in hospital. Thankfully, none of the children were killed, but four of them were wounded, by whom we have yet to determine. We do have a lot of the hotel's customers in custody, most of them having been arrested after being caught in compromising positions. We are aware that the hotel took in regular guests as a cover for their main operation, and we are determining who those are, as they are totally innocent.

We can't take any questions at the moment. I just wanted to let you know personally what was going on, and the next conference will be done by one of our press liaison officers in two hours time. By then, we will have a lot more information for you, including the number of fatalities we have suffered, and you will be able to ask your questions. For now, I hope you will give us a little time to speak privately with the families of our fallen comrades, who today showed truly remarkable courage, and will be regarded as heroes for the rest of time. Thank you ladies and gentleman."

Special Agent in Charge Wilson was generally regarded as a no nonsense career woman with no emotions. She was popular with her agents not because of that, but because they knew she cared about them and would protect their backs. It was very rare when she went in front of the cameras, but she did so this day because she did know some of the fallen. They were from her team. And the tears that were seen sliding down her cheeks as she made her speech were absolutely genuine, and she would shed a lot more when she told her agents husbands and wives that their partners had passed away.

It was another two days before Special Agent Danville in San Francisco learned that one of the girls had been identified as Sandy from Sacramento. The fingerprints and description matched, although with all the drugs she'd taken, her looks were very different.

Just as she'd done with her friend Ashley, she asked for Sandy to be transferred to San Francisco to undergo her lengthy recovery, and it was agreed upon. Special Agent Danville had also known some of the fallen in Las Vegas, and she too was grieving their loss. She had requested leave so that she could attend the funerals.

Despite all the law enforcement personnel wearing bullet proof vests, and some with helmets as well, it had been no protection against the armor piercing bullets that the gang liked to use. It had turned into a bloodbath inside the hotel, with eighteen gang members killed and ten from the various agencies. The FBI alone lost four, with five still in hospital, and the SWAT team was also decimated. Forensics had to call in for help with all of the processing, and it was still ongoing.

There was a lot of debate going on about the raid and the amount of bodies, and some of the uneducated were of the opinion that it was all handled wrong. No one should have died in their opinion, and they were even debating about whether the hotel should have been targeted. It was ridiculous, but when law enforcement are faced with people who shoot first, then there are going to be fatalities. However it was dissected, there wasn't an alternative method to disarm the gang members, and there was no way anyone could ignore that there were children being exploited and needed to be rescued. Just as Ashley had been.

Ashley was doing well now, still recovering, but getting there. Her brothers Greg and Will visited her as often as they could, helping Ashley so much just by being there and not judging her. Ashley was going to recover.

Sandy would also recover with the right help and support, and by now the correct assistance was given whereby the children could continue their lives, damaged, but not totally broken.

CHAPTER 26

Lexie by now, hated Seattle and wished she'd stayed in Portland. Her 'owner' said he was called L.J., and he'd renamed Lexie, 'Katie,' as he said she reminded him of a famous actress. He didn't elaborate, and 'Katie' didn't ask him to, she just wanted to escape. Sometimes, she would step outside after a customer had left, for a look around, but couldn't see any other way out other than past the motel office that always had someone in it. Her bathroom had a window, but it had bars on the outside, so one of the only plans that she had come up with, was to escape in a customer's car. If she could talk one into it.

She hadn't been given any drugs yet, but was warned on many occasions that any disobedience would lead down that road, and she was wise enough to not want to become a junkie.

L.J. and his friends were brutes. They'd all taken advantage of her and forced her to be compliant, and she hated them with every ounce of her being. The customers as well. She hated the smell of them, their sweat, the tacky aftershave, and she wanted to vomit each and every time one of them came through the door, with the same perverted grin.

A woman, Bella, who said she also worked for L.J., had gotten some clothing for her, but it was all for the benefit of the customers, along with some make up, bathroom supplies, tampons, perfume, and wipes.

Lexie guessed that other girls or women were in the same boat as she, but apart from the one that had got her some supplies, she never met any, but heard through the thin walls other regular sexual encounters. It disgusted Lexie, but it seemed to delight the customers who wanted to compete with neighboring yelling and bed rocking.

Most of the time, food and drink was brought to Lexie in her room, but sometimes she was also taken to a local diner. She always tried to attract someone's eye when she was in there, and if her guard was pre-occupied she would mouth "Help me," to anyone who looked at her. It had almost gotten a couple of guys in bother, as her guard had asked them very threateningly, "What the fuck you lookin at Mister? You want some trouble?"

So far, she had never seen a cop in the diner, and she wondered if she would have the bravery to run to one. There had been one occasion when a cop car pulled up outside, but then her guard had hastily dropped money on the table and they had left before the cop had even gotten out of his car. That had been the only close chance she'd had.

A Mexican maid cleaned the room every day and changed the soiled sheets and towels, but Lexie didn't speak any Spanish, and the maid always kept her eyes averted. Lexie thought the woman knew what was going on but didn't want to get in the middle of it, and if she was illegal, it would only get her deported.

The customers came in all shapes and sizes, and sometimes it would be a couple, male and female, who Lexie thought were really perverted.

Lexie began to have second thoughts about trying to coerce someone to help her. She thought it might make her plight even worse, as she could be imprisoned by one of them, and even killed. She was determined not to give in. Her life had to get better sometime.

The customers were told that they couldn't take their cell phones into the rooms, or any weapons, yet Lexie always looked. She was quite prepared to dial 911 or start shooting at everyone. There were also no pencils or notepaper in the motel's room, but there was a bible, and one day Lexie stole a pen from a customer's jacket pocket when he went to the bathroom. Once he'd left, Lexie tore a sheet from the bible that had a blank side, and wrote a note.

"Please help me. I am being kept against my will in the Sunrise Motel, in room 118 by the people who bring me in here and by others, and I'm made to have sex with many different people. I am only thirteen.

Please give this note to the police, or call them and read them this message if you don't want to get involved. This is not a joke.

PLEASE HELP ME!"

Lexie very carefully folded up the note into a small square and hid it in the bathroom cabinet for the next time she was taken to the diner. She didn't know if she would have chance to pass it to anyone, but the waitress always gave her sympathetic looks and maybe would do something if she got the message.

It was a couple of days before Lexie was taken there again, and she secreted the note inside the strap of one of the g-strings she now had to wear. She was taken there for an early dinner and she could barely eat her meal as she waited for her opportunity. It never came. As a last desperate measure, when she and the guard left, Lexie dropped the note on the booth seat out of sight of the guard, and left it there to be found and read.

The diner employed a busboy in the evenings, and he saw the note when he went to clear and re-set the table, and he opened it. Only problem was that he couldn't read English, only Spanish, so he crumpled it up and put it in with the rest of the garbage.

Lexie expected the police to knock down her door down and arrest the people who were doing this to her, for days afterwards. She imagined them sitting in their cars watching, identifying people, and waiting for the go ahead to move in and rescue her. But it didn't happen, although at least the waitress hadn't ratted on her, even though she was obviously working for L.J. and his friends.

It was another several weeks before Lexie was given an opportunity.

She'd been taken to the diner for lunch and her guard had said he was starving before they entered. They ordered their food, and just as it came to the table, two cops entered the diner and sat down in a nearby booth to the one that Lexie and her guard were in. The instruction for when this happened, was to leave enough money on the table for the food and a tip, but to leave as soon as possible. If their food had just arrived, they were to ask for to go boxes and then leave. Her guard was too nervous to leave, so keeping his voice down he told Lexie, or Katie as he referred to her, to keep quiet, or she would be hurt. They would eat some of their food and then leave.

Once they'd eaten most of their meal, the check was put on the table and cash was put on top of it. The guard slid off his seat in the booth and waited for 'Katie' to do the same. She didn't budge. She saw the anger and consternation building on his face as he gritted his teeth and said,

"Come on Katie, we need to leave now. Your Mom will be wondering what's taking so long."

It was her now or never moment. If she couldn't get the cops attention, or if they didn't believe her, she would be going back to her room in the motel for a beating, probably a drug injection, and then more awful stuff until she lost her will.

"I AM NOT GOING BACK TO THAT MOTEL ROOM MISTER WHOEVER YOU ARE. I DON'T KNOW YOU AND YOU ARE NOT ANY RELATION OF MINE. I AM THIRTEEN YEARS OLD AND YOU ARE FORCING ME TO HAVE SEX WITH WHOEVER PAYS YOU. I AM STAYING RIGHT HERE."

Everyone in the diner stopped what they were doing and were looking at the scene of the slutty white girl and the big black man, who was now attempting to drag the girl out of the booth, and one of the cops stood up.

"Is there some kind of problem here?" He asked.

"YOU'RE DAMN RIGHT THERE'S A PROBLEM. THIS GUY WANTS TO DRAG ME BACK TO A MOTEL ROOM WHERE I'LL BE BEATEN BLACK

AND BLUE, DRUGGED, AND THEN MADE TO SUCK SOMEONE'S COCK. I AM ONLY THIRTEEN YEARS OLD, AND I WAS SOLD TO THEM BY SOME DUDE FROM THE BUS STATION."

The cop moved forward towards them as his partner also stood up.

"Is any of this true?" The cop asked the man, seeing the panic in his eyes.

"No man, I don't know where she gets it from. Come on Katie, it's time for you to go home to your Mom," he pleaded, sweat pouring down his face as he tried to grab her arm.

"MY NAME ISN'T KATIE, IT'S LEXIE. I'M FROM PORTLAND AND I RAN AWAY FROM A FOSTER HOME. I DON'T KNOW YOU AND I HAVE NO MOM. WHY DON'T YOU TELL THIS NICE POLICEMAN HOW YOU RAPED ME JUST THE OTHER DAY," Lexie shouted again.

The cop moved closer and noticed the man back away, toward the exit, his right hand going around his back. The cop pulled his gun and his colleague moved around, pulling his own gun as he did so.

"Just stay where you are sir and let me see your hands. Maybe there's a simple explanation to this, so lets sit down and remain calm. Now let me see your hands."

It was the other cop who saw it first, yelling, "HE HAS A GUN!" Then he fired before his fellow cop could possibly be shot.

The noise of the gun going off at such close quarters made everyone's head ring, and the rest of the customers and staff ducked down, as if they expected bullets to start flying everywhere. They didn't, as the man had been knocked backwards, losing his gun in the process, and the other cop ran toward him, kicking the gun on the floor further away, as he held his own gun pointed right at his head.

"Don't move you son of a bitch," he told him, as his friend, the shooter, came around to check if the man was dead. There was already a pool of blood beneath him, but the cop got onto his radio and asked for an ambulance immediately, that there was a cop involved shooting, the name of the diner and the address.

Lexie too had ducked down, and she was still cowering when she felt someone sit opposite her.

"I think you'd better tell me what's going on Miss," she heard, before slowly sitting up and looking at her guard lying on the floor, and then at the cop who was now sitting across from her.

So she told him. Everything she knew in all its grisly detail, and a woman who was nearby cried on hearing the story. Halfway through the story, the cop got onto his radio and told them there was an ongoing situation and that back up was needed, along with social services and vice. Lexie continued with her story as sirens were heard approaching and then vehicles parking, and the cop asked the crying woman to sit with Lexie until social services arrived, as he went outside to talk to someone. The woman did so, putting her arm around Lexie, telling her, "It will all be all right honey, they can't hurt you any more."

As some vehicles arrived, they very quickly drove off again, and the guard was put on a gurney and driven away at speed. All the customers and diner staff were ushered out of the back entrance and were interviewed. Lastly, so was Lexie and her new friend, by a woman detective and a lady from child services. Lexie was taken to hospital by the detective and child services, without doing an interview, her clothing was cut away, and she was medically examined before being put into her own room, with her two companions following her on each step.

Once she was comfortable, she made a complete statement to the detective, witnessed by child services.

L.J., along with his cohorts and motel was closed down. A couple more minors were found, both addicted to drugs, along with several adult prostitutes and some customers. The cops had no idea this had been going on, right under their noses, and admitted that if Lexie hadn't had the courage to make a stand, then the operation ran by L.J. would have gone on indefinitely. Now, he was looking at a very long prison sentence that would keep him behind bars until he died.

Lexie had internal injuries that would heal, after surgery. With the description she gave, the cops were able to identify and arrest Jess. He was charged with human trafficking, and he also was looking at a very long prison sentence.

The woman who had consoled Lexie in the diner became a regular visitor to the hospital, as Lexie made her slow recovery. She introduced Lexie to her husband and children, who Lexie really liked and was liked by in return. Even when she volunteered the information about stealing money from her last foster mother and running away.

After very careful consideration and an emphatic and unanimous vote, they filled out all the forms and asked social services if they could adopt Lexie, and to foster her until the permission to do so was approved.

Lexie's life was about to get way better.

CHAPTER 27

In the suburbs of Chicago, a young brother and sister had gone missing. The Violent Crimes against Children Unit in the Windy City were looking for them, and especially the woman who by all accounts had lured them away. And many others. The only thing they had to work on was that she was tall, in her early thirties, long wavy blonde hair, green eyes, high cheekbones, slender figured, and damn good at what she did. The woman didn't mind using her female wiles to obtain things

These days, the woman went by the name of Gina Flowers. A fake identity, but to all intents and purposes a real one. Everything she used now was in that name. Driving license, passport, social security, insurance, credit cards, et al.. For the assistance she gave to the traffickers, in return for money and sexual favors, she had easily obtained her new identity, a little plastic surgery on different parts of her body, and the trust of those who were important.

Her day job was selling high end cars, and because she was so good at it, she didn't have to work a full week. The sales personnel she worked with gave all sorts of reasons for Gina being better than them, and it was usually sexual. She did use her assets, especially on test drives when the buyer was alone, but ultimately she could sell and everyone knew it. Other car dealerships would continually make her offers to join their sales teams, but she had a good deal where she was at, especially from the financing of the vehicles. That's where the real money was made for the sales team, by getting the customer to agree to a finance deal with the dealership, rather than with an outside company. Cars were still sold for cash, but not as much money was made, although the trade in prices they offered were a joke. Everything was designed to make money for the dealership and the sales team. Not to give a good deal to a customer, just make them think they were getting a bargain.

Gina was good at spotting customers too. The normal tactic in a car dealership was to approach a customer as soon as they set foot on the lot, offering to help, giving them a business card, suggesting a test drive, asking their price range, and what particular type of car they were looking for.

Gina rarely did that. Instead, she loitered around until she was approached, and then she knew she had them. If she went after a customer, it was harder work, and depending on what was said, she would often give them a different salesman's name card, knowing full well that no sale was ever going to be made. Gina preferred to sell to the guys who were alone, but if they were with their wives, she would flirt seriously with the female. She usually found that the woman would be flattered, the husband intrigued at the thought, and sometimes the woman would slip her their number.

Single women were the toughest to sell to. They could smell a bad deal a mile away, so to get them in the car of their choice, more haggling needed to be done. They also wanted to know more about details rather than performance, miles to the gallon rather than the fastest speed, the color of the car and its interior being a good match to them. Gina had the men on that aspect. They never even thought about good hiding places for purses, or if the pedals were too far away from the feet. Gina would actually steer women clear of certain models because they weren't designed for women drivers, especially small women, and doing that gained people's trust. Very often, someone would come into the dealership and ask for Gina, not wanting to deal with another sales person. That would drive the others crazy, as they watched customers waiting for their turn with Gina.

She only worked there for three or four days a week, depending on what her other cash only job was asking her to do.

Gina had been married once and hated talking about it. That was in New York. They'd had two children, were doing well, and were quite the envy of their friends and neighbors, as they always seemed to do things effortlessly and were nice to know.

Although Gina was married and enjoyed having sex with her husband, she also liked having sex with other women. Her husband knew about it from when they first met, and he loved it when Gina suggested a threesome with him and one of her women. He would brag about it at work and show his friends the pictures of the other women that he bedded, with his wife joining in or watching.

Then one day, after working late and missing a dinner reservation for an anniversary, he went home and found his wife making love to the babysitter they had hired for the night. As he undressed to join in, the young girl said she didn't want to have sex with a man. Gina told him to go away, she was mad at him for forgetting their dinner date, and so he left them to it. He had a few drinks too many, and as he listened to both females orgasm, he called the police.

The upshot was that Gina was arrested for rape of a minor, was convicted, and her husband got full possession of the children. Gina was classed as a sex offender, had to serve time, was made to wear an ankle bracelet on her release, and forced to report to the police station every week. Gina hated it. So as soon as she earned some money, she cut off the bracelet, and moved to Chicago.

She looked in on her kids sometimes, from a distance, after taking the train down to New York, but it was very upsetting to her. Her husband had now re-married, and although she thought many times of setting him up, she knew it would be the kids who would pay. Gina had told the cops when she was arrested that her husband had on many occasions had sex with minors, but they didn't seem to care, and ultimately it was Gina who did the suffering.

The only thing that seemed to alleviate her pain, was recreating the sex she'd had with minors previously. Back then, they had been willing and wanted to learn, but even though the ones she now had sex with weren't the same, she found she enjoyed it, and it felt like she was getting her own back on her ex-husband, who probably missed his threesomes.

Her job for the traffickers was picking up children, and Gina never gave a thought to whatever happened to the children once she handed them over. She was always allowed her own time with the girls she picked up, which she took, but she never touched the boys. Something inside her made her think that the boys would be much better adults if they were gay. She didn't trust heterosexual men, who would cheat on their partners to have sex with her on a test drive, or had betrayed her trust, or sent her to prison.

The tactics she used on the children were varied. To Gina it was like selling a car, and the first thing anyone bought was herself. The secret was to find what kind of person the customer wanted to buy. Be it sexy, demure, worldly, exciting, trustworthy or whatever. But it had to be done quickly, so reading them was of the utmost importance.

Children were no different. They might be looking for a friend, or someone to love who would return that. Maybe a little excitement. Perhaps something illegal. Fun. Money. Tickets to a concert or sport game. Spoken to like an adult. A makeover or new clothes. To be allowed to drive. All kinds of things, and Gina knew how to discover what they yearned for.

The last two had been really easy. The boy and the girl had been sitting on a park bench, their legs swinging because they didn't reach the ground. Both looked miserable as Gina approached them and asked if they minded her sitting down. Taking their lack of comment as a 'yes', Gina sat down and took out her iPad and some candy. The boy was next to her with his sister on his right, and he watched Gina as she opened a game and kept losing. Gina didn't say anything, but she knew the boy was getting agitated with how useless she was at playing the game. After several more failures at the game, the boy felt forced to speak.

"You know you're playing that game all wrong don't you?" He commented in his little man's voice.

Gina looked down at him as if she was seeing him for the very first time.

"I just can't get the hang of it," she replied, with a little frustration.

"I can show you if you like, it's very easy really." The boy was itching to play the game.

"You're not going to run off with my iPad are you? Someone did that to me before, and I've only just got this one."

"No, don't be silly, I just want to show you how to play the game is all."

"Well, if you're sure. I don't trust many people these days," replied Gina.

"You can trust me," said the boy, "now let me show you how to play."

Gina handed over the iPad, and she watched as the boy showed her how to play the game. Gina took a piece of candy and then offered the two children some. Which they took.

"You see how easy it is?" The boy asked her, as his fingers flew over the screen.

"It might be for you, but my hands don't move as fast as yours. Are you as good as he is?" Gina asked the girl.

"No, but he plays games all the time. We're not supposed to talk to strangers," the girl replied.

"That's good advice. My name is Susan, I'm harmless, and now that you know my name, I'm not a stranger. Can you tell me your names, otherwise I won't be able to talk to you. I'm also not allowed to talk to strangers," said Gina, smiling. "And I will have to take away my iPad if I don't know you."

"Not yet please," replied the boy, "I'm heading for a record score! My name is Dylan, and my sister's is Abby."

"It's nice to see a brother and sister together in the park, but why aren't you playing on the swings or something? It can't be much fun talking to me on a bench," commented Gina.

"We were told to come and sit here," said Abby. "Mommy and Daddy were having a fight, so they told us to come here for a while before going back home."

"I'm sorry, have you been here long?" Asked Gina with concern.

"It's been a while, but we don't want to go home too soon in case they are still arguing," added Abby.

"I can understand that. So while you wait, I have an idea. As soon as Dylan here ever finishes my game, why don't you come and have an ice cream with me? I don't normally eat ice cream, but you two kids are my perfect excuse for having one before I have to go home. What do you think?" Asked Gina.

The two kids looked at each other before deciding yes.

Gina wasn't too worried about being seen with the children. It was rare for an ice cream parlor to have security cameras, and even if they did, Gina wasn't known around this area. If someone did come up with a description, it wouldn't matter, as she was in disguise.

Like all good sales people, Gina knew she had her customers and it would take very little to close the deal. Although Abby was a little younger than Gina preferred, she was very cute and Gina was looking forward to teaching her. She didn't care about the boy. Someone else would deal with him, and Gina was expecting a bunch of cash coming her way.

Purely to keep the children quiet, they were drugged before spending the night in the backseat of Gina's rented car, and she kept them drugged until they reached their destination. Gina handed the pair of them over, spent her allotted time with Abby, and never gave them another thought. She already had her next order and was eagerly anticipating the hunt.

The parents of the children actually thought they were blameless. They thought they were doing the right thing in sending their kids outside while they squabbled, then making up, before actually going to see if they were okay. The police, who had been the first responders, could hardly believe their stupidity, but it didn't stop them searching. Nor the FBI when they took up the case. Apart from a vague description of a good looking brunette they had nothing.

Nobody saw Dylan and his sister Abby ever again. They were gone. Gina still eludes the law.

CHAPTER 28

Close to the Big Pine Lake in Minnesota, a religious cult had been preparing for everything from a civil war, to an invasion by the Chinese. The leader and founder went by the name of Charles Miller, had inherited multi millions from his deceased parents, and believed virtually every conspiracy theory going.

After purchasing thousands of acres of land near to the lake, he had a company construct what looked like an old fort in the middle of the property, but with more modern amenities. Generators, solar panels, working bathrooms with their own water supply from a well, televisions, movie theater, library, pool, and connections to a mains sewer. If something was to happen, which Charles was certain of, then they would revert to chemical waste. Apart from the surface buildings, there was also an extensive fortified basement with it's own generators. The underground compound was continually being stocked with guns, ammunition, long shelf life food, bottled water in case the well was compromised, chemicals, living accommodations, short wave radios, dvd's, gas masks, night vision goggles, bullet proof vests, flashlights, batteries, air purifiers, clothing, medical supplies, games, tools, gas, books, cd's, and everything else to self sustain.

Around the fort were farm buildings for the sheep and cattle, farm machinery, and a church.

The church was very important as Charles was an ordained priest, and all his land and buildings were now recognized as a religious retreat for his own particular religion. A big part of the religion was being able to have many partners, male or female, at whatever age Charles decided they were sexually capable.

Not only had other adults joined the 'church', they handed over their money to contribute to the cause, and worked the fields and the cattle. In the evenings, after prayers, they would not only swop partners, but would also take advantage of the children that Charles bought, but also the ones sired by the followers.

On Sunday's, their day of rest, everyone would attend church to listen to Charles's main sermon, which concentrated on the demise of the human race, how they would soon be alone, and that they would have to defend themselves against the forces that would be determined to take everything away from them. Everyone would have to stay alert, keep doing their arms training, and protect their extended family. Nearly all the sermons were a variation of this, with Charles picking up on news that he thought was suspicious, and dangerous to their way of life.

Apart from the fort, the whole encampment was fortified. No-one could enter the land without passing through an armed and always manned gatehouse. The outer fences were high and were entirely of razor sharp wire, with many cameras covering them and always monitored for invaders.

The local people didn't like them at all. The few they saw who would go into town to literally empty shelves, gave them the creeps the way they looked at everyone, especially the children. They all dressed alike, the men in identical black jeans, boots, white v necked undershirts, and plaid shirts. All the men were clean shaven, had their hair cut by a number two razor, and always smelled of musk. Both males and females sometimes wore white baseball caps with the 'church's' insignia on the front, which was an outlined naked family wrapped around a cross. Nobody within the town liked the insignia. The females had their own uniform. All their hair was cut to the same level, just reaching the neck, tight blue jeans, black boots, black tops with sleeves. In the summer they went to sleeveless white tops but kept the jeans, presumably to work in. The women always smelled the same, and although they weren't plastered in make up, they all sported smoky eye shadow, and pink lipstick.

Unbeknown to the townsfolk, cleanliness was very important to Charles Miller, so everyone around him had to appear neat, to look good, smell nice, and to shave their whole bodies every day, including the men, or use a cream to prevent body hair. It wasn't an all white community, but everyone had to adhere to the rules, so the African Americans amongst them had their hair straightened or shaved.

There was no age limit to the followers, but with the farming it kept everyone fit. Even the resident doctor and dentist had to stay fit, so they would often be seen jogging or in the small gym, along with the three cooks.

They had a communal dining room and everyone ate together at the same times, apart from those on security duty. If anyone got hungry between meals, then there was fruit and raw vegetables available, and coffee and tea could be had anytime, along with water. Virtually everything was communal, except the unlocked plain bedrooms, which was to protect the other sleepers from the snorers.

Charles had added a vineyard to the fields of crops. It wasn't in the most ideal of places, but it provided a wine that was very drinkable, and in the evenings everyone could imbibe.

Apart from everyone having their own jobs and duties, and because it was so communal, jealousy was not tolerated or any fighting. There had been occasions when someone had gotten into a rage about seeing someone having sex with another, which had incurred threats and violence. Charles then had to step in and banish them. It rarely happened, but when it did, he was quick to sort it out.

Charles Miller looked like all the other men. He didn't set himself apart, except he didn't work the farm or the fields, and he was the only one to have a computer and internet connection. He also had a cell phone but very rarely used it, and if he wasn't in his office, he put it in the safe along with the computer. Probably the only thing that really set him apart, was his vivid blue eyes. It gave him presence. He was by now in his late thirties, looked younger, had never been married, nor had any of the community, as it was considered a 'possession'.

He wasn't sure if he had any children. Although birth control was used, sometimes one of the women was allowed to have a child but not with one particular man. If a woman requested to become pregnant, she had to have sex with a number of the men, and when the child was born the mothering would be shared, apart from the breast feeding. So it was quite possible that Charles had fathered many times, or not at all.

The most unique thing about the commune, was that everyone in it liked to have sex with everybody, be it man, woman, or child. They also liked to observe and join in if invited. Charles preferred the children above all else, especially when he first purchased them or the homegrown had aged a little.

He had turned it into a coming of age. Watched and assisted by the community, he would be the first to take the child on the altar in the church, and when he was done, he would assist as someone else followed him. He called it their spiritual birth and acceptance into their free world. Once it was over, they would all bathe and gently caress each other, proclaiming their love and devotion.

Nobody seemed at all bothered or perturbed about Charles having a computer or a phone. If they ever asked him to call a family member or something, he would gladly do it or even do research for them. They all loved their lives, and whenever there was a dispute, Charles would sort it out like he did with the jealous ones. He kept the actual punishment details to himself. Normally, with a small dispute, just the threat of banishment was enough to stop it. If it went further, then he would publicly banish them, then take them in one of the vehicles to a very remote area and shoot them dead. Tying heavy rocks to them, he would roll them into a nearby small lake, watching to make sure they slipped under the surface and didn't reappear.

He didn't want someone he was throwing out running to the police out of malice, and telling them what went on in his carefully crafted fort. Like his followers, he liked his life, and he wasn't ready to get into a gun battle and have his life ended. So when he brought out the banished, he told them that before he took them to the bus station, he needed to speak to them in a place that he felt was spiritual, with no distractions to their calm discussion. They were dead before they knew it.

Although Charles had plenty of money, the farm was also making money. The walk in freezers were kept full and rotated with fresher meat and produce, but there was still a lot of leftover, that Charles was easily able to sell. Once the civil war started, or the invasion happened, or the bombs started dropping, there would be nothing more to sell as they retreated to the basement with whatever they had, along with the chickens. Cash then would be of no worth, so Charles was stockpiling gold to replace his assets. He felt he was ready for anything, and with all the guns and ammunition he had, they could keep anyone at bay for a very long time.

He had recently purchased, and had just taken delivery, of four children from the Far East. Three very young girls from Cambodia, and a little boy from the Philippines.Tonight, he was going to indoctrinate the first girl into the ways of the church, and then do the same to the other three on the following nights.

Some of the women would hold and console the girl as Charles lubed and then raped her. Everyone would give their encouragement to what was going on, to prevent the child from screaming and struggling. They were also anticipating their own turn.

The children weren't picked up by Charles personally. He had one of his more trusted men do it, in return for being second in line with the first indoctrination.

No one knew outside the gates, what went on inside the fences, but they didn't trust them and wanted the police to get rid of them. They police wished they could, but the religious aspect prevented them, and there was no evidence of any wrong doing to get a warrant. Stockpiling legally bought weapons and ammunition, along with dried and canned foods, was no offense.

CHAPTER 29

Hannah was being raised as a Mormon in Salt Lake City. She had been adopted at a very young age after her biological parents were killed in a car wreck. She had survived the crash and had ultimately been taken in by friends of her parents.

Hannah had a lot of issues, most notably being an orphan, and was always being reminded of it at school and in social media. It wasn't her fault a sleepy truck driver had plowed into them, instantly killing her mom and dad, but that didn't stop the other kids from picking on her and calling her names.

She was eleven now, not the prettiest girl in the world but neither was she the ugliest. It may have helped her to apply a little make up like the other girls did, but her new parents didn't allow her to do that as they didn't agree with it. Hannah was a little nerdy as well. She would much rather work and play on her laptop rather than do sports, and she wasn't interested in getting a boyfriend or gossiping. At school, she mostly got A's or B's depending on the subject, and didn't cause any trouble.

At her new home, she felt a little isolated from the family, like she was a guest rather than a sister or daughter. She also wasn't keen that her new father believed in corporal punishment if any of the kids did something wrong. So if Hannah got a B- or worse, she got the back of her legs smacked, and was told to do better next time.

A couple of times Hannah had tried to run away, usually to her old home, which was now occupied by someone else. When she returned to her new home, or was found, then there was more punishment.

Hannah had sad brown eyes, limp brown hair that stopped at her shoulders, good healthy teeth, a nice dimpled smile when she showed it, and was beginning to get acne. Every night she put cream on the upcoming spots, which sometimes worked, but often didn't.

She had no affinity with her new brothers and sisters, there were a few of them, and one of the girls was her chief tormentor along with her friends. Hannah really wanted to leave.

She had found some websites and chatrooms for kids like her, who had been adopted or fostered. They seemed to be like herself, they were unhappy, and everyone related their tales and looked for answers or advice.

Some of the kids talked about meeting someplace, in the different cities they lived in, and getting to know each other face to face. Other kids talked about way outs that were available, like sponsored boarding schools for computer programming, modeling, and acting. Some of the kids said they'd enrolled in these schools, and it was the best thing they had ever done. Once they had been to check out the schools, firstly alone and then with their new parents, it had been an easy process, and with being sponsored by wealthy backers everything was available to them.

Hannah checked out the web links they attached, and it all looked cool. Nobody was saying bad things about these places, it was all good, so she clicked on one of the links and filled out the form that came back, returning it electronically.

Getting a reply, she was asked to meet up with one of the tutors, a Ms. Romney, in a coffee shop Hannah knew of in Salt Lake City, not far from the university. Ms. Romney would be wearing a short mauve jacket with a flowery scarf tied around her neck, but if Hannah got cold feet then she was under no pressure to meet her. She could just walk away and think nothing more of it.

She met Ms. Romney three days later right after school, and immediately liked her. Ms. Romney told her to call her Dee, she was in her early thirties, had black, combed back hair to her scarfed neck, wore gold earrings, a necklace with a cross, and a had a nice warm smile. She was attractive and warm.

When Hannah introduced herself, Dee stood up and shook her hand, and asked Hannah if she'd like something. Dee herself was going to have another latte, so Hannah asked for a frappuccino. Hannah sat down as Dee went for the drinks, and she brought back a couple of cookies as well.

Dee took off her jacket before sitting back down, and Hannah noticed how nice her hands looked with the long fingernails.

"Well thank you Hannah for meeting me here today. It's very nice to meet you and I hope we can arrange something for you."

Dee had a soft voice. It was audible, but it didn't carry.

"Nice to meet you too Ms. Romney," Hannah replied.

"There's no need for formality Hannah, you can call me Dee," she smiled, before continuing after looking at her open screen on her computer.

"I am so sorry that you are in a poor situation Hannah, with your adoptive family, and I'm sorry too about the circumstances that brought this about. I myself am an orphan, but I never knew my parents, so I can only imagine what it was like for you to lose yours in such tragic circumstances."

Hannah didn't reply.

"Let me tell you a little about our program Hannah. It was set up by very wealthy people who wanted to give something back, and in particular to orphans or fostered children. They too were orphans, who had a miserable upbringing, but after becoming rich they got together, and came up with this very special program. Of course, there are tax benefits for them in doing this, but their primary purpose is to help the less fortunate.

You probably looked at the links on the website, but here are some more photos for you and some literature that tells you more."

Dee handed over a folder that had been lying beside her computer, and watched as Hannah browsed through them.

"We have many facilities around the country Hannah, as you can see from the photos, but here in Salt Lake we have acquired an old school that we have completely refurbished, and we are currently filling the classes up. It also acts as a residential home, so all the children have their own rooms and bathrooms, communal areas to eat and to play, and we have an indoor swimming pool and media rooms. Whatever you want to specialize in, be it computers, film making, fashion, or whatever, that becomes your main subject, and all the subjects that need to be done, like English and math, revolves around your main focus."

Dee had Hannah's full attention, and she pointed out the photos from the Salt Lake residence.

"Do you have any bullies, or punishments if the children do something wrong?" Asked Hannah.

"I'm glad you asked that Hannah, because it is something close to my heart. We don't tolerate bullies at all. We keep a close watch on all the children, and if we see or hear anything untoward then we take action. All the tutors are instructed to listen to the children, and if someone mentions to one of the tutors that they or someone else is being bullied, picked on or whatever, then they must act. We have had bullies, but they were all expelled and sent back to their homes. As for punishment, we don't believe in physical hurt, but obviously, if someone does something wrong then there has to be consequences. It all depends on the situation, but it can be detention, being made to go to your room, denial of television or computer usage, or even being expelled in the worst situations. It really depends on what was done."

"Okay," said Hannah, "so how do you convince my adoptive parents that I'd be better off elsewhere?"

"That's a great question Hannah, and we don't always convince them. Most of the time we do, but not every time. We used to take the children and the parents to the school together for the first time, but we found that either they would back out, or they would talk themselves out of it before we even got there. So now we take the children first, and if they like what they see, then we have an ally when we take the parents. Of course, some children change their minds, but on the whole they love what they see and hear, and when they talk to the parents it's with a lot of persuasion. So nowadays, we ask the children to come and take a look first, and if they don't like it, then they don't even need to even mention it to their parents. It's a very delicate thing Hannah. Parents don't like to hear that their children want to live elsewhere, and they don't want to hear that their child has already taken a look. So until you see the school with your own eyes, it's better that you don't mention it. Don't you think?"

"Yes. I would probably get my legs smacked if I mentioned meeting you Dee, and I know I'd be smacked if I told them I'd been to see the place."

"Do you get smacked often?" Asked the concerned Dee.

"Enough. So when can I come and see the school?" Replied Hannah, not wanting to talk about the smacking she received on a regular basis.

"Well, I could take you now, but I do need to be back soon to meet someone else, so it would be a quick trip rather than a detailed one. So what do you say Hannah, would you like to take a quick look?"

"Yes, I would if that's okay. I'm already late getting home so another few minutes won't make much difference."

"Then let's hurry Hannah."

Dee got all her things together and led the way out to her Mercedes parked around the corner, and they drove away.

They drove for about thirty minutes to an area that Hannah had never been to before, and then Dee took a turn down an obscure lane where they came to a guarded gate.

"We have this gate Hannah to protect the children. This is a very secure property and we want to keep everyone safe."

Dee had already got her window down as they approached the guard.

"Hi Charlie, I won't be here long. How are you?" Dee asked pleasantly.

"I'm good thanks. You look great as always Dee," he replied flirtatiously, as he raised the gate.

Dee waved as she drove through, and down the tree lined lane.

When they came to the very old school, no one was around, but the grounds were manicured and the school looked well maintained. It was six levels high, the walls were stone, and there were many chimneys atop the roof. Steps led up to the main entrance to two huge solid wooden doors that were closed, but one began to open as they climbed the many steps.

The woman who opened it was about the same age as Dee, but to Hannah she looked like she was about to go to bed, or for a shower, with the pink bathrobe she was wearing. She also wore a lot of make up, particularly around the eyes and her black eyelashes were very long.

"Hi Dee, the gate said you were heading down here. Are you staying long?"

"No, I have to get back, but I should return in a couple of hours. This is Hannah by the way."

"Come on in Hannah," the pink robed woman said, moving aside to let her in.

It was only when the door closed behind her leaving Dee outside, that Hannah got worried, even more so when two huge men appeared and blocked the door.

The woman looked down at Hannah and said, "Now let me tell you what really happens in this school that Dee neglected to explain. This is now your home Hannah, so you need to get used to it."

There were no school rooms at all. Apart from the living areas at the top of the house, the whole building had been turned into movie studios. Scenery, furniture, beds, cameras, lights, fake staircases, kitchens, all kinds of different scenes. Hannah was taken into a room and told to stay very quiet, then was made to watch as a scene was filmed for a movie, a man getting a blow job from a naked woman. Even in the basement pool that had scenery to make it look like it was outside, two women were making out in front of the cameras, and then when Hannah was taken upstairs, she guessed what was in store for her. A man with a girl about her own age, being filmed from all sides.

"You'll get used to it Hannah," the woman told her. "I did and now I make really good money. You may even become a star."

CHAPTER 30

Alice and Ray Phillips had tried for years to have a child, but nothing ever happened. They underwent tests to determine if anything was wrong, but all seemed in working order, so they tried herbal remedies, different positions, odd locations and times. Ray would rush home when Alice was going through her menstrual cycles, but it all seemed to no avail.

They were just a regular couple who got by. Ray worked for a satellite provider as an installer and Alice was a cashier in a megastore. Neither earned a great deal of money, but they figured that because they didn't splurge on anything, that they could afford to have children to complete their family.

Both were born and raised in Topeka, Kansas. They didn't know each other growing up and only met in their early twenties when Ray went into Alice's workplace to buy some work clothes, along with some groceries, and Alice was at the end of the checkout line that Ray was in. It was an instant attraction, only enhanced by the lack of wedding rings on both their hands.

Alice was a pretty woman, with wavy brown hair and blue eyes, small nose, and a warm smile. She was plump though, which wasn't helped by sitting at a register five days a week and her fondness for chocolate and pastries. Ray though didn't mind that. He didn't like skinny women, much preferring a woman with curves who didn't feel guilty about it and Alice fit the bill.

Ray too was no adonis. Although he climbed a ladder most days to install satellite dishes, he liked to eat, drink beer in moderation, and wasn't keen on keeping fit with exercise. In looks he didn't get many backward glances, with his full cheeks, brown eyes, and receding dirty blond hair. Most of the time he wore his company baseball cap, jeans, tee shirts, was a pleasant man, and he and Alice were keen fans of the Chiefs and the Royals.

They lived on the outskirts of the city, where the homes were cheaper, but in a very decent neighborhood with little crime. Ray drove a beat up Ford truck that he perpetually worked on, and Alice had a Honda Civic that was very reliable, but far from new.

Doctors, friends, and family would often ask why they didn't try a surrogate, or adoption, or whatever. Some of the things they couldn't afford, but they didn't want to do others, preferring to leave it to nature and their Christian beliefs. If it wasn't meant to be, then they could live with that.

So when Alice announced that she had missed a period it came as a great surprise, and one that they didn't believe until the time that they actually saw their baby squirming around in a scan. Even then, Ray couldn't make out what was on the screen until it was pointed out to him.

Alice was almost forty when she became pregnant, and had never thought it would actually happen after all the barren years. She thought when she was younger she was ready for a baby, had it all planned down to the finest detail. Over the years of disappointments, the preparation was all forgotten, so she and Ray went into overdrive to get things ready for their child's arrival. They knew it was a girl from the scans, but that didn't matter in the slightest. They were finally going to be a Mom and Dad.

Ray and Alice doted over their newborn. They named her Mira, short for the miracle they both thought she was, and she was a beautiful blue eyed blonde. Although they tried, Mira was to be their only child.

Mira was as pleasant as her parents. She gained many friends, and her infectious laugh delighted everyone. At school she was an average student, but her parents didn't push her, and she loved to dance. Her parents took her everywhere to watch and learn, and they loved seeing her prance around the house practicing her moves.

Just after Mira had her tenth birthday, she went out of their lives. She vanished off the face of the earth. Mira had wanted to go and see a movie so they happily took her, and when she said she wanted to go to the restroom, alone, as she was all grown up now, they allowed it and waited for her to return. Except she never did.

Despite having an amber alert, and a security camera picking up Mira being held by the hand of a woman in a large hat, she was never found. No clues, no trace, no body.

Alice and Ray were totally devastated. Never in their wildest dreams had they envisaged Mira being taken by someone. Not being able to find solace at church, the only thing they had to cling on to was that her body was never found. It seemed that everyone told them that Mira was probably buried somewhere, but neither felt that she was dead. They believed that because they were so close, they would know if she was gone, so they kept her room as it was, and always kept a light burning to welcome her home. They looked of course, everywhere they could think of, and would show her picture to anyone who would look. No one had seen her, but they kept the light on.

It was ten years before there was a knock on the door, and an FBI agent, one who looked familiar, asked to come in. Hearts sinking, the now much older Ray and Alice sat down to hear the news.

Mira had been found alive. Before the agent could explain the circumstances, Ray and Alice were already hugging and crying, and it was a good five minutes before he could tell them the rest of the story. Mira had been found in Reno, working on the streets as a prostitute, was very hostile to law enforcement, and was going through drug rehab. As she was an adult now, it was very difficult to charge anyone for what had happened to her as a minor, and she wasn't saying anything anyway. Mira had no I.D., she wasn't in good shape when she was picked up, thinks she's called Cindy, wants to be released back onto the streets, and doesn't, according to her, have any family.

It didn't matter in the slightest to Alice and Ray, they just wanted to see her and to bring her home.

Mira had been in rehab for months and was still angry. The cops, or the FBI or whatever, kept saying she had family, and that her real name was Mira Phillips and she was from Kansas. Mira thought they were all stupid and that there was no such place as Kansas. Even when her parents arrived Mira couldn't remember them, but Alice and Ray's enthusiasm, combined with their dogged determination, began to seem familiar to Mira, and as she looked through the mountains of photographs, things began to fall into place.

Ray and Alice were told that it would take a lot of time for Mira to come to terms with what had happened to her, but that with the right support, she would recover. In one respect, she was lucky in that she hadn't picked up an STD and would still be able to have children one day, although surgery was required to repair some damage.

When they were finally allowed to take her home to Kansas, Alice changed her shift so that one of the parents was always home with her. Getting back to her own room was very therapeutic to Mira, as she looked through her drawers and her old clothing and toys. Although Ray and Alice wanted to get her a bigger bed, Mira asked them to wait as her old one felt comfortable, but she did agree to lots of new clothing.

Alice felt like she'd been reborn as she took her daughter shopping, and as Mira had missed so much school, her parents found a volunteer tutor who came to their home. Slowly but surely, Mira recalled how she was taken away, even the movie they had gone to see. Blaming herself for going with the nice woman, who had said she needed help with her sick pet dog who she'd left alone in her car. The woman didn't know if the dog would be dead or alive on returning to her vehicle, so Mira had gone with her.

Mira didn't remember much after getting to the car, just the first drug hit and being raped the first time. Then it was all a blur until she was arrested and started the drug withdrawal, when she felt so sick.

Like a lot of recovering victims, Mira wanted to work in child services once she was able, to help others try to recover from their abuses.

CHAPTER 31

Stephen Crane, George Matthews, and Jake Darren thought they had it made. Three very young girls who no one was looking for, and who they could do whatever they wanted to with. Jake kept a close eye on all and any police activity, and Stephen had the money to keep purchasing them. As for George, he was the perfect fall guy for Stephen and Jake, while George himself was just happy to be able to indulge his fantasies.

The three little girls could put up with George and Jake. It was terrible, but compared to Stephen, it was the easier option. Stephen liked to hurt them, and the louder they screamed the better he liked it. Taking one of the girls into his cage, the other two would be forced to watch, which he liked, his depravity knowing no bounds.

When Jake or George came over, either singly or together, Stephen would happily watch on the close circuit and wonder how they could get so much pleasure without causing a lot of pain. Stephen was by now building up to his crescendo. He had been informed of another auction that would be happening soon, and with money not being an issue, he would buy replacements. It was the ending that always gave him the most satisfaction. Everything beforehand was foreplay to him, and although he greatly enjoyed it, ultimately he wanted the climax.

Sometimes he would watch the recordings of his previous climaxes, remembering the girls and his actions, the terror on their faces as they realized they were going to be killed by this sadistic monster.

The girls had realized that Stephen secretly watched them, as he would suddenly appear if they were huddled together talking, or if one of them was rummaging around. They had though managed to find the exit to the outside.

It had been camouflaged by paneling in the closet, and it was only because one of the girls felt a draught when she was sitting on the floor, that it had been found. Stephen would turn all the lights off during the night when he went to bed, and during this time the girls would take it in turns to pry open the panels. Although they had no tools, they had plastic kitchen utensils which they utilized to create an opening. Because of their small body size, they only needed to remove two of the panels, and once they had done so, they wedged the panels back before the lights came back on.

Behind the panels were cobwebbed stone steps, that led up to double doors that were on a forty five degree angle. They wouldn't open, so the girls had been working on the hinges, with whatever they could find, smelling the cold fresh air outside as they toiled in the darkness.

One night, after Stephen had turned off the lights, they bolted.

Not having any shoes made it painful, but after what they'd been through it was a tolerable pain, as they ran down the long dirt lane away from the farmhouse. Getting to the road, there was no traffic, no street lights, just a little moonlight, as they debated whether to go left or right.

Deciding to go right, they ran again, beginning to think it was futile until one of them noticed a light just further on. It was a house set back off the road, but not far, and the light was in a window. They opened the garden gate and sprinted to the front door, banging on it and ringing the doorbell, until they heard yelling inside and more lights coming on, as someone approached the door.

They still didn't really know much English, just the instructions they'd learned, so when a man, and a woman behind him opened the door, the man brandishing a shotgun, they thought they were going to be killed. They huddled together, waiting for the loud explosion from the gun.

"What the fuck," stated the shocked homeowner, as he looked at the three girls and then at his wife, who could barely believe her still sleepy eyes. She stepped out from behind her husband, trying to see beyond them, thinking their parents must be close by. Her husband still had his shotgun aimed directly at them.

"Put the gun down Chad, can't you see they are little girls. But what they are doing out here and dressed like that I'll never know."

Hello!" She addressed them. "Is there something we can help you with?"

None of the girls budged or spoke back.

"Who are you? Where have you come from?" Asked the woman.

"Maybe they don't speak English," said Chad. "They don't look like they're from here."

"No shit Sherlock, I would never have guessed," replied the sarcastic wife. "But look at how they're dressed, and neither of them have any shoes on. Something is very wrong here Chad, we need to call the police."

Chad gave the girls a good look, in their flimsy clothing, the dirty and blood stained feet.

"What do you think happened to them Chris?"

"I don't know, but I don't think it was good. Let me try and get them inside while you call the police, and call social services as well. We can't send them back to their parents if this is how they treat them."

Chad went back inside to make the calls as Chris, short for Christine, gently tried to usher the girls inside and out of the cold air. She managed to get them into the family room and they sat together on the couch as Chris realized how young they were, and what a pitiful state they were in. She handed them a couple of throws and turned on the gas fire, as she tried in vain to communicate with the Asian looking girls.

"Mom, what's going on?" One of Chris's daughters had appeared at the open door to the living room. Her name was Julie, and like her mother, was dark haired, blue eyed, narrow in face, and wearing pajamas. She was about the same age as the girls.

"I don't know dear, these kids appeared out of nowhere banging on our front door. Your Dad is calling the police to see if they have any missing children."

"They look scared stiff Mom, did something happen to them?"

"We don't know. Maybe the police have been looking for them or something. Can you make them some hot chocolate while we wait? I think it's better if I stay with them."

"Okay, I'll make one for me as well."

Julie passed her Dad on the way to the kitchen and told him what she was doing. He was still holding the shotgun.

"The police are on their way and social services said they would send someone over when they could. The police don't know of anyone missing so have no idea who these girls are. God, they're so young, how could anyone not know they were missing?"

"I don't know Dad, but did you see how they are dressed? And no shoes? I don't think they speak any English either."

By the time a siren was heard, the girls were drinking their hot chocolate and beginning to calm down from their shaking. Julie and Chad met the cop at the front door, explained what had happened, and then took the policeman into the family room.

It was like a bomb went off.

Immediately, the mugs of hot chocolate went flying, the girls screamed and ran toward the kitchen, and when Julie and Chad caught up, they were brandishing knives and trying to open the door to outside. Terror was on their faces as the cop approached them, telling them to put down their knives.

"I don't think they speak English," Chris told the policeman.

"They speak enough. I'll take them home now," he stated.

"You know where they live? You want to take them home when they're dressed like that?" Exclaimed Chris.

"They always doing this", explained Officer Jake Darren. "Just not this far from their home. I'll take them home now and you folks can go back to your beds."

As the cop slowly advanced on the girls, they looked for all the world like they were going to stab him, until Jake pulled his gun.

"You just pulled your gun on three little girls," said the unbelieving Chris.

"We'll get going now," replied Jake, pointing at the girls to drop their knives and lead the way out. "They won't bother you again."

Chris looked at the girls faces. It was a mixture of absolute fear, dread, and hopelessness. She, her husband and daughter, could only watch as the girls got into the rear of the squad car and then leave, all three girls looking back at them through the rear window.

"This isn't right Chad. What on earth have we done?"

Chad had put down his shotgun when the cop arrived and now wished he hadn't, he was as distraught as his wife.

"What else could we do?" He replied, as they watched the cop car disappear. As they did so, another car came from the opposite direction and pulled to a stop. A woman stepped out, smartly dressed in a suit, but her hair was unkempt.

"Hello. I'm Janice Rawlings from Child Services. I came as quick as I could but as you can see I'm still in a mess. Are the three girls still here? Can I speak to them please?"

Janice seemed very pleasant and warm.

"The cop has just taken them home," replied Chad.

The expression on Janice's face totally changed to one of anger. She looked at the notes she'd been carrying in the poor light from the porch.

"I was told the three girls were shoeless, were dressed inappropriately, didn't speak English, were around eleven years of age, and their feet were bloody. Is that correct?"

"Yes, but the cop said he knew who they were, they did this all the time, and he was taking them home. But one thing did bother us," replied Chris.

"What was that ma'am?"

"He pulled a gun on them."

"He did what?"

"He pulled a gun on them."

"Oh Jesus," she replied. "How long ago did they leave?"

"Just seconds, you almost ran into the back of them."

"Who was the officer?" Janice sounded urgent now.

"He didn't give us his name, but the girls were petrified at just the sight of him."

"How did the girls get here?" Asked Janice. "You don't seem to have many neighbors around here."

"We think they walked, or ran. Their feet were a mess. The only neighbor we have is a couple of miles in that direction," Chris pointed, "the same way the cop car headed. But we have nothing to do with the guy who lives there, he gives us the creeps."

"Why is that?"

"Just the way he looks at you, especially the kids. I don't know of anyone who likes him."

"Is he married?"

"No. He lives in that old farmhouse all alone."

"Okay, I need to go. You say it's a couple of miles to his house?"

"Yes, but you're not thinking of going there are you? Not alone? Won't the girls be home now?" Chris asked with concern.

"If there were kids around here who perpetually ran away in skimpy clothing I think I would have heard about it by now, and it's not a cop's job to put minors in their car and take them home to possibly abusive parents. I think I should just check out your neighbor before leaving."

"Then Chad will go with you, and I insist. We could never sleep again if something happened to those kids, and we didn't like the cop pulling his gun on them. Chad, go and get your shotgun and take this lady to that creep's house next door."

Chad was obviously used to doing as he was told, and ran and got his shotgun.

"This is very kind of you Chad. Do you think you could drive while I make some phone calls?" Janice asked when he returned.

"Sure, no problem. I didn't want that cop to leave."

Janice handed over her keys to Chad as she immediately got on her cell phone, the two of them waving at Chris and Julie as they sped off.

As Chad got to the long lane leading up to the farmhouse, Janice broke off from the phone to tell him to cut the lights and the speed as it may well be a futile journey, and she didn't want an angry owner on her case. She then went back to her conversation as Chad crept up the lane. It wasn't until they were almost at the house that they could make it out, and just one dim light inside. The cop car was at the front door and it was empty.

Janice broke off from the phone again to tell Chad to back up to the entrance to the lane, and as he began to slowly reverse, he heard her telling someone to get there a.s.a.p. or if not sooner. She was still on the phone as he got back to the road, and she told him to block the lane with the car, to get out of the car with her, and they'd wait for help to arrive.

Chad wished then he had gotten dressed rather than still be in his pajamas and nightgown, but thankful he wasn't in just his usual boxer shorts. He still felt stupid as they waited behind a tree, dressed for bed with his slippers on. At least he had his shotgun.

Although there were no trees alongside the lane up to the farmhouse, there were trees on the road so the car did block the route to the farmhouse. Chad wondered what the cop would do, and looking up the lane he saw the headlights go on the squad car, and it started to make its way down the dirt lane. Chad was wondering if he would get into a gunfight with the cop. It was eerily dark and quiet, and they would have to stop him leaving somehow. He wondered if he could aim his gun at a cop and shoot.

The cop pulled up at the abandoned car, got out of his, and looked around. He tried the doors, which were locked, then looked around some more, wondering what was going on. Then he, along with the hiding Chad and Janice, heard the sirens. A lot of them.

Jake ran back to his car, and putting it into drive he began to ram Janice's car. He was trying to spin it around by concentrating on one corner, and he was almost on the road when the first squad car arrived.

Jake thought he was okay then. It was a fellow cop, who would just let him get on his way, and he got out of his squad car and ambled over to his colleague. His colleague got out of his car and pulled his gun, telling Jake to get to his knees, to keep his arms up, and to go face down. As Jake tried to reason, the other cop repeated his instructions, forcefully, as more squad cars arrived and more guns were pointed at Jake.

Jake did as he was told, then felt the hands on him taking his gun and pulling his arms behind him and being handcuffed, as others frisked him for another weapon. At that point, Janice made her presence known along with Chad's, and taking the keys back from Chad, she moved her badly damaged car out of the way, before talking to someone in a suit.

Chad thought it was all very exciting until he was told to remain where he was and his shotgun was taken off him. He then watched as a fleet of vehicles went up the lane to the farmhouse, quietly, with no lights flashing.

Inside the house, the very angry Stephen was unaware of what was going on outside as he prepared the cage in the cellar. He was spreading plastic sheets everywhere to catch the blood and lessen the clean up. In particular, he didn't like this part to be rushed and Jake appearing in the middle of the night with the three girls in his backseat had forced this upon him. Jake had told him that they had made their way to the house next door, and only God knew what the girls had said. Stephen thought that he might need to take the neighbors out as well, but if he had to, then he would make sure their daughters paid. Right now, he had work to do and needed to do it quickly. The sheets all in place and his tools ready, he grabbed one of the girls, muttering, "This is going to hurt me more than you."

The girl was struggling, yelling and screaming, so he hit her hard on the chin. Then for good measure, he caught the other two girls who'd ran in different directions, and knocked them out as well, throwing their bodies on to the beds to await their turn. He strapped the first girl down and sighed in disappointment at having to forego his usual ritual, before placing his strong hands around the little girl's throat.

Stephen was so deeply into it, he never even heard the cops running down the steps and telling him to let go. It wasn't until he felt the cold steel of a gun on the back of his neck that he knew his time was up, and he released the girl from his grip.

The cops yelled for paramedics as they checked for a pulse on the strapped down girl, one of them starting CPR as others kept shouting, until the medics appeared and they took over. Janice was summoned, as Stephen, now handcuffed and aware of his rights, was put in the back of a cruiser. She was able to sit with the two girls who were recovering consciousness, as their friend was put on a gurney.

The man in the suit approached Janice and stood away from the beds.

"Good job Janice, but what made you call us all in? This could have been a job ending situation if you'd been wrong."

Janice looked around and shrugged her shoulders, but not releasing her hands from the two girls.

"I just knew something was very wrong. Three tiny girls in lingerie arriving at someone's home in the middle of nowhere, not speaking any English, petrified of a cop who waved his gun in their faces, and who then drove them away before anyone else arrived. It was practically a no-brainer."

"Still, it took guts to go against a cop. I'm proud of you Janice, well done. Is there anything I can help you with?"

"No, not really. These girls have been through hell so it's them that need the help now. You could have someone take Chad home. He's the guy in the dressing robe at the end of the lane with a shotgun. He deserves to know what happened here. He and his wife are the ones who saved these girls, not me. If it wasn't for them, they'd be dead now, and we would have nothing."

"Okay Janice, consider it done. I'll catch you later."

The man in the suit, who was a Special Agent with the FBI, left Janice with the girls, as he checked with his agents who were collecting evidence.

Officer Jake Darren tried to make a deal, but because Stephen Crane had been so meticulous with his recordings, his pleas fell on deaf ears. George Matthews never even tried to deal. He'd had his fun and expected to pay. Stephen Crane never admitted to anything, but he had left video evidence that showed him killing twenty one girls. No bodies were ever found, he hadn't filmed their burials, but everyone wondered if there were more.

Stephen Crane was put on Death Row to be executed by lethal injection, and Officer Jake Darren along with George Matthews was sentenced to life imprisonment with no possibility of parole.

The three girls, once they went through extensive care, learned English and were granted citizenship, along with a new life with loving adoptive parents.

Chad and Chris were lauded as heroes in town, but thankfully, they found sound sleep again.

CHAPTER 32

Janelle was still in love with Michael but she still hadn't grasped the fact that he was using her. She may well have thought she was all grown up, but in many respects, she was still very much a child.

Michael kept telling her on the nights he stayed with her, that it wouldn't be long before they would go away together, but despite all of Janelle's help, he was still in debt, and they needed extra money to go away with. The import business wasn't doing very well still, but things were definitely looking up, and it was just a matter of time.

He would tell her over and over how much he loved her, so she had no reason not to believe him, and she would do anything for him.

Janelle didn't like the strange men entering her room or what they did to her, but when one man had hit her, hard, Michael had beaten him to a pulp. Janelle witnessed it, liking that Michael told the man that this is what happens when he messes with his girl. To Janelle, he was her knight in shining armor.

The diner that Janelle and the other girls ate in was never really busy, but it acted as a front for Michael's business. Although he never worked in it, he owned it, and the few staff he had run it, were well paid and very scared of him. So they turned a blind eye to the girls, would try to keep them apart, and would also send the johns to the rooms after they chose the girls and paid. As for the motel, that was owned and run by a cousin of Michael, who tried to stay as ignorant as possible about what was going on. Sometimes, a regular guest would complain about the continuous sex going on next door. but he would just shrug his shoulders and say "Sorry, I can't forbid them not to, but I can change your room."

The maid knew what was going on as well, but she needed the job, and none of the girls seemed to be bothered about what they were doing.

Michael was doing very well financially. It seemed to him that there was an endless line of men who wanted to have sex with a minor, including himself. He'd been a pimp for women before doing minors, but it was nowhere near as lucrative and they were always complaining. Michael was actually older than he looked, he was now in his early thirties, but he was very grateful for looking younger as it enabled him to attract the girls.

At least for now. Being able to buy girls when they entered the country meant that he didn't have to rely solely on his looks.

He'd brought Janelle in when one girl had gotten too old for the clientele. She was only eighteen but hardly anyone wanted her anymore, so he sold her to another pimp, after telling her to get her things as they were going to start a new life together. He didn't like handing her over, but business was business.

Unknown to Michael, the vice squad were closely watching his operation. They had received a tip from a motel guest that a young girl who was next door to them, was having sex with much older men. Different men. The vice squad made a few inquiries and then did a short surveillance, noting that there was indeed something going on. Photos they took of the customers were of convicted sex offenders, and until then, people not yet on their radar.

Detective Davis, Sam to her friends and Samantha to her mother, had been trying to chat with one of the girls without revealing her identity. The only place she saw any of the girls go to was the diner, and she already knew that their pimp owned it. She had been in once or twice for lunch, had been able to sit by one of the girls at the counter, but had still not had a conversation. The diner had been just too quiet to not get noticed. So she bided her time, watching the motel from a safe distance and the comings and goings, until one morning the diner seemed to get a rush on for breakfast. One of the girls had already left, but two were still in there, sitting well apart at the counter top, so Sam got out of her car and went inside.

She sat at the side of the one who had gone into the diner last, which happened to be Janelle.

"Coffee ma'am?" Asked the waitress.

"Yes please, and can I have some cream?" Replied Sam.

The waitress pushed over a bowl filled with individual half and half's, grabbed the coffee pot and a mug, and poured. The menu had been on the counter when Sam sat down along with a knife and fork on a napkin.

"Do you know what you want or do you want a couple of minutes?" The waitress asked, as behind her, steaming plates were placed on the shelf in the hole through to the kitchen and someone yelled, "Lori, you're up!"

"I'll have the two egg breakfast with Canadian ham please, with whole wheat toast," answered Sam, handing the menu over.

"How do you want the eggs?"

"Oh, scrambled please."

As the waitress left to attend to someone else, Sam poured some half and half into her mug and took a sip as she glanced to her left. Janelle was dressed in an almost there skirt, a blouse only half buttoned revealing a white bra beneath it. Sam herself was in jeans, a blue top, and a light blue jacket that concealed her gun. Her brown hair was tied at the back with a scrunchie, and she looked like a kindergarten teacher. Janelle was just getting her breakfast, some pancakes with bacon, and she was pouring maple syrup over the stack.

"That looks good, maybe I should have had ordered that," opened Sam.

Janelle looked at her neighbor, but didn't say anything.

"Whenever I've been in here before it's always been quiet. Where have all these people come from?" Continued Sam.

"From the motel I think, across the street," answered Janelle shyly.

Sam thought the girl was around thirteen or fourteen, but was trying to act older.

"Of course, I never thought of that. Do you work near here?" Asked Sam, knowing full well school had already started and didn't want to infer that she knew Janelle was a minor.

Sam's breakfast arrived and the waitress asked if she needed anything else, after sliding over a plastic container that had ketchup, hot sauce, mustard, steak sauce inside it, along with salt and pepper. Sam shook her head no as the waitress poured more coffee and left the ticket. There was no ticket in front of Janelle.

"I work for my boyfriend. We're going to go and live in Florida soon," Janelle stated proudly.

"My boyfriend is a jerk, he has no ambition, no nothing. I'm thinking of dumping him," Sam responded.

Janelle hadn't really had a conversation with anyone but Michael, or the staff here at the diner for what seemed like forever, and she thought it was nice that someone just wanted to gossip with her.

"Then you should, there's no point in just staying with him. My boyfriend has a lot of ambition, he's just struggling at the moment with some debts, but we'll be fine soon."

Sam guessed rightly that was how her pimp controlled her. It was an old trick that still worked, and it was obvious that the young girl was in love with him. They continued eating and chatting.

"That's good. Was it business problems?"

"Yeah, but he says it's improving now."

"What kind of business is he in?"

"He imports and then he sells. Just hasn't had the right stuff lately and got into debt. Soon though, we'll be off to Florida."

Sam knew it would be futile to try to turn Janelle on her pimp, she would defend him to the end, but at least now she realized how much work would be needed to convince Janelle, how fooled she'd been. Sam engaged her in other conversation, like television and movies. Janelle knew about some shows but hadn't been to the movies for quite a while, so didn't know what the latest blockbusters were. Sam liked Janelle, she was just a girl who needed love and thought she'd found it.

Several days after Detective Davis spoke with Janelle, the diner and the motel were closed down. Michael was arrested, along with the diner staff and some customers caught in very compromising positions. The girls defended Michael to the hilt, even the two who didn't speak much English.

It was only when the vice squad let each of them see and hear the other girls, that they began to question things. Michael had told them all the same story. The nights he spent with the others corresponded to the nights he was absent from their own beds, and gradually, they came around. Two of the girls were from Cambodia, and had basically learned English from watching television. An interpreter helped to get their story, which was that they'd been taken from their homes and then put on a container ship. After arriving in the USA, they were dressed up, and then the next thing they knew, they were with Michael. At first he'd been forceful, had beaten them, but then they got to like him and he started spinning his story about how he had gotten into debt and that he would take them away once he was able. The two girls hadn't known each other, had seen one another, but both believed that they were the only love of Michael.

Janelle was devastated and wouldn't believe it at first, saying it was a trick by the police to make her think badly of Michael. She kept insisting she was eighteen and knew what she was doing, so they could just let her go.

With the diner getting closed, Sam was able to convince a couple of the servers to make deals, telling them that otherwise they would be charged as accomplices along with the diner staff. Michael was going to be labelled a sex offender, and that he was looking at very many years behind bars for his various crimes, which were federal.

Sam kept away from Janelle until the truth hit her, and Child Services said she would be able to handle a conversation.

She actually looked like a little girl again when Sam introduced herself as a cop. In the diner they had never exchanged names, but with Janelle's statements, and some checking, Sam now had her whole sorry story.

"Hi Janelle, nice to see you again. My name is Samantha Davis. I'm a detective with the vice squad, and what I told you about my boyfriend was true. I took your advice and dumped him."

Janelle looked at the detective sitting opposite her, and tears began to fall down her cheeks.

"How could I be so stupid?" She asked, wiping her face with the palms of her hands.

Sam moved over to sit with her, and gave her a hug.

"You are not stupid Janelle. You got taken in by a man who knows how to lie. I'm a cop and it happened to me. If you're stupid, then so am I."

"Then I guess we're both idiots," Janelle laughed and sobbed at the same time, her tears wetting the jacket that Sam was wearing, as Sam rubbed her back.

"You'll get over this Janelle. Sure, it will take time, but this happens to very many girls and when we rescue them, they are usually drug addicts, riddled with diseases, and have lost years of their lives. You Janelle, have been checked by the doctors, you're free of disease, haven't been on drugs, and you know what has happened. Which believe me, is very important. You are going to be okay. You'll be able to lead a normal life, and you have a new friend who you can always call. Me." Sam slipped her card into one of Janelle's hands. "I mean that Janelle, it's not just words, I want you to be a friend. We're going to find you a nice loving home, not like your last one, and when you get settled call me, and we'll go to a movie or something. Okay?"

"Okay. Thank you Samantha. Right now I really need a friend!"

CHAPTER 33

Jenny had been imprisoned for ten years, had given birth to two children, yet she still hadn't seen her twentieth birthday. She'd had a disagreement with her mother and so was waiting alone for the school bus to arrive, when a car stopped and asked her for directions. As she leaned into the open passenger door, the driver reached across and hit her hard on the nose, breaking it, and then he dragged Jenny into the car and drove away.

It wasn't even that far from her home, maybe a mile or two, but for the last decade Jenny hadn't been able to escape. On a couple of occasions she'd tried, but had been caught and been made to pay. Her captor, Marty Stevens, was a scary man, and liked to use his fists and feet on her. He was also a big man, around two hundred seventy pounds, black hair, balding, always with a stubble, and too much body hair. Jenny thought of him as a thug. Marty also had a cousin who shared his house, looked just like him, and Jenny suspected in-breeding. The cousin, who was called Brian Maddox, was as bad as Marty. The two men were of a similar age, around forty now, and Jenny was petrified of them.

Jenny used to get annoyed with her Mom for not being allowed to do things her friends were doing. Like staying out longer, having unsupervised sleepovers, eating different things, watching certain movies, having private chats on the web. At the time, Jenny would get so mad, yelling and slamming doors, and that led to her being left at the bus stop alone as her mother stormed off.

Now she realized how stupid she'd been. She didn't blame her mother at all for leaving her at the bus stop, as she had been out of control and she knew it. For ten years she'd been waiting to apologize for her behavior, and to promise never to do so again.

Jenny still remembered all her school friends and her small brother, wondered how they were doing, and if they missed her as much as she missed them.

Jenny had never been drugged and had been able to watch television and listen to the radio. At the beginning, Marty and Brian would laugh at the news of Jenny's disappearance, giggle at her Mom pleading for her return and her Dad in tears. There were no descriptions of Marty or of his vehicle, and the police kept pleading for anyone who may have witnessed something, to come forward. No one did, and the news died down very quickly. Jenny would continue to watch the news in hopes of hearing her name, but eventually gave up on that, as it only caused despair.

During the times that Jenny wasn't being raped or abused, she could roam around the house if Marty or Brian were there, cleaning the house and doing laundry. When she was wanted by one of the men, it would be in the cellar, the attic, or in one of the bedrooms. There, she would be chained, roped, or handcuffed.

By now, Jenny was a pleasant looking woman, not the gawky kid she once once. She wasn't allowed any make up apart from deodorant, but her brown hair was now long, her skin clear after begging for acne removers, and she was lean from a bad diet and malnutrition. Her two little girls were also thin but otherwise healthy, and she never, ever, wanted to go through childbirth again.

Jenny had been alone for the first couple of years and then she was joined by a Latin girl called Yolanda, and later by another caucasian by the name of Kim. They were a couple of years younger than Jenny and Marty and Brian subjected them to the same torture by television. They just loved watching the news and hearing the pleas from their parents.

The house itself was far from special. It was a run down house in a poor area of Atlanta, with steps up to a full porch, two levels, an attic and a basement. All the doors had padlocks, and the windows were covered by a thick layer of plastic sheeting. One of the cousins would always be home, and if they wanted a nap then they would chain up the girls against a wall, or lock them into a room, usually the cellar as it had no windows. Yolanda and Kim helped Jenny with the cleaning, but the food was always fast food. Every day except weekend, Marty worked as a mechanic during the day and Brian filled shelves at night in a grocery store, and when they came home they would bring fast food with them. The only time they actually got real food was when the babies were born, and then it was the bottled variety for the child.

The first time Jenny got pregnant she had a miscarriage. Yolanda and Kim, along with a medical book, helped Jenny, who was devastated when the tiny baby appeared in the world dead. They also cleaned up all the blood as Marty took the baby away.

Jenny did give birth two years later, successfully, but without any medical assistance or drugs. Yolanda and Kim stepped up and acted as midwives. Yolanda and Kim also got pregnant, as the men never used condoms or gave them birth control pills, but only Yolanda had a baby. Kim had several miscarriages and Marty got angry with everyone each time. When he got angry, he beat them all.

The girls had sometimes pulled down the plastic sheeting on a window and banged and shouted to get a neighbors attention on one of the few times that they'd been left alone, but locked into a room. One neighbor had actually waved to them but had done nothing else, and time marched on.

Kim had once managed to open a kitchen window and get into the back yard, but once there the high fence with barbed wire below the top had stopped her from climbing over, and her pleas for help had only got the attention of Brian, who dragged her back indoors and beat her until she was a bloody swollen mess. Jenny and Kim thought he'd killed her, so bad was the beating, and Marty had praised his cousin when he got home, telling him he'd done a great job.

Jenny's older daughter, who Marty had named Julia, was sometimes taken out by him to visit his mother. The mother had never been to the house, at least as far as Jenny knew, and it obviously never raised any suspicions with the neighbors that Marty would be seen alone with a tiny girl. Marty would even go around to the neighbors for a beer or for a barbecue, and sometimes bring back some chicken that the hungry girls would gobble up.

For clothes, Marty would go to the goodwill store and guess their sizes, but he did have to buy diapers, menstrual pads, and lotion. The girls didn't do any school work, visit the dentist, have any books to read, or leave the house. Once in a blue moon they were allowed into the back yard, singly and under supervision, but only on a bad day when no neighbors were around.

Jenny, along with Yolanda and Kim, often thought of escape and they would talk about it among themselves, principally on how to do it. They thought about rushing one of the men, Brian, and try to grab his gun before he could start shooting, and maybe shoot him. If he was able to shoot, then so be it, their ordeal would at least be over. But whenever they thought about it, Jenny and Yolanda would think about the children, and the realization that if they were killed, then their children would have no mother.

The girls had all gotten used to the sex with the smelly, gross men, but none of them liked it when they got kinky with the chains and the ropes, hurting them until they screamed and screamed.

Nobody was looking for them now, there was never any news about them on the television or the radio, and it was very depressing to them. The two men would torment them about it, telling them they weren't loved by their families and that they were probably glad they had gone.

Brian would nearly always fall asleep on the couch by the front door until his cousin came home, and then he would go and sleep in Marty's bed until he went to work. Neither of the men ever took the girls into the master bedroom unless it was to be cleaned and the sheets changed. They were never left alone in there, and once the cleaning was done, the door was padlocked closed. Jenny longed to get her hands on the laptop and the land phone that was kept in there, but she couldn't even dust them without being told to keep away.

Jenny, being the oldest girl, felt that it was up to her to do something before the two men got tired of them and killed all three, leaving the small children to their mercy. They had to get away or at least give it another try. How would she be able to explain to her daughters, who had known nothing but this life, that she had given up. That was no lesson for them. At least if she was killed trying, then Yolanda and Kim could tell them that their Mommy had died trying to make their lives at least a little better. Jenny resolved to herself, that if any opportunity came by, she would have to make an attempt.

By the time one did, Jenny's twentieth birthday had passed by with no ceremony. The only dates the two men celebrated were the days they'd taken the girls, and Christmas. The girls hated them celebrating, as they got drunk and treated them even more cruelly.

Marty had gone to work as normal, and Brian was at home. Most of the time they had alcohol available, but this time there wasn't any and Brian was complaining that he needed a drink as he hadn't slept the day before, and he was also hungry as there was nothing in the fridge. So he locked the girls into one of the bedrooms on the second floor, and said one of them would get lucky on his return, as a good drink at the bar would make him horny.

They heard him leave, and Jenny got her courage together.

"I've got to make a run for it otherwise we're all going to die here," she told her friends and family as she tore off the plastic sheeting from the window overlooking the back yard. "If something happens to me, just remember that I did it for us all."

"What about your kids Jen? What will we do if you don't make it? There's no way out from the yard," said the very worried Yolanda.

"Can I come with you mommy?" Asked Julie. "Please don't leave me."

Jenny saw the tears in her daughter's eyes and almost gave in.

"I have to do this Julie. I'll be okay, and I'll be back for you in a few minutes. Hold onto Yolanda like a good girl. I won't be long."

The window, like all the others, had been nailed to prevent it from opening, and Kim was sitting on the only chair in the room.

"Kim, let me have the chair, and everyone protect your eyes."

Kim let her have the chair and she and the others cowered by the door as Jenny swung the chair at the window, as hard as she could. The window smashed loudly, most of the glass flying outwards.

"How are you going to get down to the yard?" Asked Kim. "There's no pipe or anything, it's just a straight drop."

"It's not too high," replied Jenny, picking shards of glass out of the bottom of the window frame.

"But you'll never get over the fence," continued Kim, who'd once tried herself.

"I have a plan," said Jenny, hoping it would work.

She guided the chair out of the window and then bending down as much as she could through the window case, dropped the chair away from the wall, praying it wouldn't fall apart. It seemed to stay intact. Then she took off the top blanket from the bed and threw that out. Gritting her teeth, she then slowly eased herself out of the window, gripping the window case as hard as she could and taking her full weight as she dangled over the drop. There was nothing for her feet to purchase, and although Yolanda and Kim could have maybe pulled her back up, she let herself go. They heard her scream as she hit the dirt below the window.

"Are you okay?" Shouted Kim through the open window.

Jenny looked up with a grimace and pain shooting through her right ankle, which she thought was sprained or even broke.

"I'm okay," she gasped.

Limping heavily over to the chair, Jenny was thankful it was in one piece still, and she dragged it over to the nearest part of the fence, standing it up. She then hobbled over to the blanket and picked it up, before returning to the chair and stood on it. Her head was barely at the level of the fence but she could at least get a good grip of it with her hands. She put the blanket over the top of the fence and over the barbed wire, and stood for a moment on her left foot as she got a firm hold of the fence. It was now or never. With a look over her shoulder at the anxious faces looking through the broken window, she leapt off her good ankle and swung her right leg over the fence. The wire tore through the blanket, she could feel the barbs on her skin, and she did the only thing possible apart from staying absolutely still. She went over the fence, feeling her skin rip in multiple places as she fell onto some bushes on her back. She had to keep moving. Leading with her still good left leg, she half fell off the bushes onto the soft grass that she'd often heard being mowed, and looking around, she saw the rear door of the house. Getting to her feet, which was no mean feat, she could feel blood running down her chest and belly, and it hurt as she limped and stumbled to the door, banging on it with all her might.

"Who's there?" A woman answered, "I have a gun and I'm not afraid to use it."

"My name is Jenny Taylor. I was kidnapped over ten years ago by the men next door and I need you to call the police. Now. Please ma'am, call the police, tell them who I am, and that lives are in danger."

There was silence for a few moments.

"Stand back from the door. I'll shoot if I have to."

Jenny hobbled back a little, seeing her blood stained tee shirt and jeans dripping blood as the door was unlocked and very slowly opened, a gun barrel pointed right at her midriff.

"Oh my God, what happened to you?" Exclaimed the middle aged black woman, dressed in a skirt and blouse.

"Please call the police ma'am and tell them my name. They've been looking for me for years," Jenny pleaded.

The woman had a cell phone in her hand and handed it to Jenny, telling her she'd already called and that they were waiting to speak to her.

Jenny took the phone in a bloody hand.

"My name is Jenny Taylor and I was kidnapped over ten years ago by Marty Stevens and Brian Maddox. I need the police here now, right now, as one of them will be back in a minute and he will kill the others."

"The police have been notified ma'am, now what is your address."

"I'm sorry if I sound rude, but I need the police here right now. Lives are in danger and I have two children in that house," Jenny told her.

"Give me that phone girl," demanded the neighbor. "Now listen here. I gave you my address when I called you and this young woman is at my back door with blood pouring down her belly, and she needs the police and an ambulance here right this second. Do you hear me? Now how long before someone gets here?" She demanded, then listened for a moment before hanging up.

"C'mon you poor thing, lets wait by the front door. I've got my gun still and I'll protect you until they get here. Is that where you got over the fence?" She asked Jenny, looking over her shoulder at the blanket on top of the fence and the crumpled bush.

"I'll get blood all over your floor," replied Jenny ignoring the question.

"That's alright girl, don't worry about it. I think I hear some sirens, can you get to the front door?"

"I don't know, my ankle's in a bad way. Can I use your shoulder please?"

"Honey, you can use both my shoulders. Come on, I think someone just pulled up."

They made their way slowly to the front door where a cop was waiting on the front porch, and before he could say anything, Jenny was telling her story, the names of the men, where they were, who was in the house, and how scared she was of them. The cop got onto his radio as Jenny sat down, her new friend right beside her, promising nothing more would happen to her.

Almost before anyone realized, the whole street seemed to be swarming with police and unmarked cars, ambulances and neighbors wondering what was going on. They were used to seeing cops in this part of town, but not like this. Jenny was being attended to by paramedics at the same time as the cousin's front door was being forcibly opened.

The first cop had now been replaced by a Special Agent Russell, who was listening to Jenny's tale as well as informing her of what was going on, telling her that Marty Stevens and Brian Maddox had been apprehended and were now unable to hurt her. Within seconds, everyone seemed to be standing around in total amazement as Yolanda, Kim, and the children came out of the front door, running to Jenny as the paramedics put her on a gurney, kissing her and holding her hands, thanking her for what she'd done.

Jenny had indeed broken her ankle, needed very many stitches from the barbed wire, but felt the pain was well worth it. She was finally out of there, and was going home to her family. They could barely believe it when they were called by the FBI telling them to go to the hospital as their Jenny had been found, and Jenny's mom held her like there was no tomorrow, and introduced herself to her granddaughters.

Kim and Yolanda had the same kind of reunion with their families, and although they all had to stay in hospital for several days to undergo many tests, no long term physical harm had been done to them, despite the repeated beatings.

Human remains were found in the yard of Marty Stevens house, and as he and his cousin had caused the miscarriages, they were also looking at murder charges and death row. The whole city was in disbelief that three kidnapped children had been held for so long and so near to where they had disappeared from, and the neighbors of the two cousins couldn't believe it. They'd noticed the windows covered in plastic sheets and the amount of fast food they'd taken inside, but had never wondered about it. As the media asked more and more questions, the more the neighbors felt worse at not spotting something was wrong, and for just keeping to themselves. When one neighbor proudly came forward to say that he had waved at some girls who were in the attic, everybody inwardly grimaced.

CHAPTER 34

Charles Miller had endured a couple of difficult days. One of the men had really mistreated one of the little girls, so much so that she had to be treated by the doctor and was now confined to bed. Some of the women were taking it in turns to be with her, and nurse her through the pain. Everybody had been furious with the man for what he did to her. It was understood by everyone that they needed to treat the young girls gently. Some of the women did enjoy rough sex, but even they were appalled at what had happened.

After a hastily convened meeting, at which the man didn't seem, or want to admit he had done wrong, Charles made the decision to banish him. The man was very annoyed at this, but everyone else agreed with the leader.

Charles took him out the following day and the man complained all the way to the spiritual place by the lake. He just didn't see that he'd done wrong, he was sorry he hurt her, but he couldn't help it as he was just too big. It wasn't his fault, it was just one of those things. When Charles mentioned that it was a rule not to have rough sex with any of the children, the man again proclaimed his innocence, saying he wasn't aware of the rule and that the girl enjoyed it. Charles knew that wasn't true, the poor thing had been screaming in pain and blood was pouring out of her. The doctor had to stitch her up after administering tranquilizers.

Charles had him sit down on a large boulder as he walked around, pretending to be contemplating and getting spiritual guidance. All the time Charles was watching and waiting, and when the man became still and quiet, looking away from Charles, he pulled his gun from the back of his pants, and calmly walked over and shot him him in the back of the head. Gathering some heavy stones by the edge of the lake, Charles retrieved some rope from the car, and after dragging the man down to the lake, tied him up with the stones and rolled him in. After the pockets of air finally dissipated, the body sunk into the depths of the small lake.

Charles slept with the mother of a young girl that night. He needed to persuade her that her daughter was now ready for full involvement with the group, and that he wanted her on the altar soon. The mother was thrilled to sleep with Charles. Everybody loved Charles but very few got close to him, and she hadn't slept with him for some time. Charles had learned from observing all his disciples what they liked, so unlike his previous encounters with her, this time he really pleased her. He waited until the dawn of the morning before telling her that her daughter was now ready, and was expecting a disagreement. Instead, she agreed and thought her daughter had been ready for a while, and that becoming an adult would curb her unruly behavior. Charles said he would be very careful with her, and asked if there was a special favor he could do. They went back to his bed.

The girl wasn't at all happy with her mother, so Charles had other women hold her down and soothe her as he took her virginity. By the time she was placed in the communal bath, the girl was broken and no longer yelling at her mother.

In town, Sheriff Pearce was dealing with a farmer he didn't particularly like who was insisting that his cattle were being poisoned by something in a lake alongside his property.

"Why on earth are you letting your cows drink from the lake Jessie?" The sheriff asked with annoyance. "That can't be good for anybody, never mind your cows."

"I can't stop them sheriff, there's no fence there and it's never been a problem before. It's a freshwater lake. But now they're getting sick and costing me a fortune with the vet."

The sheriff felt disgusted as he realized he'd probably eaten parts of Jessie's sick cattle.

"What do you expect me to do about it Jessie, put a fence around the lake for you?"

"You could at least check it out, see if something is in there like a container, or something that's leaking. It's not as clear as it used to be, there's something wrong. The vet will tell you that my cattle are sick, and if someone is dumping chemicals, then where next?"

"It's not like we have a diving crew Jessie. Who the hell do you expect to jump into a lake? Me?"

"What about that fireman who scuba dives on his vacations. He could go down there couldn't he?"

"Let me think about it Jessie. Where on the map is this lake anyway?"

The sheriff pulled a map out of his drawer and laid it on his desk, and Jessie eventually found the spot.

"It's right there sheriff, that's the one," Jessie said excitedly.

"Okay Jessie, leave it with me and I'll see what I can do. Now if there's nothing else you can go, as I'm already late for my dinner."

The following day was quiet so the sheriff wandered over to the nearby fire station. The firemen were standing around chatting as he approached, waiting for the alarm to go off.

"Hey guys," he addressed them all, "does one of you scuba dive?"

When one of them admitted to his hobby, the sheriff related the story that Farmer Jessie had told him the previous night, and to just shut him up, he wanted the fireman to go into the lake and keep the farmer from complaining. The fireman agreed as long as the sheriff's department would cover his costs, like cleaning his wetsuit and filling his tanks.

The sheriff agreed with a grunt, and after the fireman returned from his home with his gear, the sheriff led the fire crew to the small lake.

Everybody just kind of stood around as the one fireman put on his wetsuit, wondering what the hell they were doing there around the murky lake, glad it wasn't them who was going to get immersed in it.

Fully suited, the fireman gave everyone a thumbs up and put his feet into the water, finding the bottom and started to walk, slowly getting submerged as he walked downwards, and he put his mouthpiece over his mouth to breathe. Even with the very bright flashlight he'd brought with him, it was difficult to see anything, so about the only thing he could do was feel.

On the banks of the lake, the fireman's colleagues watched with the sheriff as the diver went beneath the surface, and waited for him to return with whatever he found down there. If he returned. It seemed like a long time to the audience before he emerged, covered in reeds and mud which raised a few chuckles from his friends. Taking off his mouthpiece and goggles, he was all serious as he said, "I need some ropes guys. Sheriff, you've got a crime scene here. There's bodies in there with rocks holding them down."

"Bodies? How many?" Asked the worried Sheriff.

"A few, at least from what I could make out. It might be a better idea to drain the lake rather than drag the bodies out. It isn't very deep, there's just a lot of mud at the bottom."

"Sounds like I need some help with this one," said the dejected Sheriff. "I'll make some calls as you guys pump out the water. I don't want to be the one who ruined evidence by dragging out bodies. Pump it out guys," he ordered, as he went back to his car.

Before long, another fire engine had arrived along with a bunch of people from the FBI who weren't looking forward to the very messy job that awaited them. Three pumps were now operating, and every so often one of them would get clogged up. With supervision from the FBI, they were cleaned out and the contents gone over by the forensic team.

Slowly and surely, the bodies became visible, even those submerged in the mud. After many photographs, each body was carefully removed after the rocks were cut away, and they were rinsed off by the firemen before being taken into the large tent that had been erected by the FBI. The sheriff was in total disbelief. He didn't know of anyone who had gone missing apart from one asshole of a husband who had left his wife with all kinds of debt, yet here were all these bodies.

Special Agent Martinez, who had been detailed to the find, made his way from the tent to the Sheriff's car and sat in the passenger seat. Despite his name and being able to speak Spanish like a native, the agent was pure American. His ancestors had moved to the USA very many years ago and although he retained Latino looks, with his black hair and brown skin, when he spoke it was with a mid west accent. In his forties now, he was still slim thanks to a regular fitness routine, and he was craggy rather than handsome. The sheriff on the other hand was overweight, smoked and drank too much, and a big white stetson normally covered his balding head.

"I need you to come and look at some bodies Sheriff, see if you know any of them."

"Okay, but like I told you before, there's no one missing in my town that I know of."

"I still need you to take a look. From what we can determine at the moment, all the victims were executed by a shot to the rear temple, with the same calibre of weapon. The odd thing is that all the men are wearing the same clothing, and the women are as well."

"There's women victims?" Asked the sheriff.

"Three of them, along with eight men. This is a dumping ground sheriff."

"It's no wonder the water was bad."

"What do you mean?"

"A farmer complained yesterday that his cattle, who had drunk some of the water from here, were getting sick, that's why we came out. Let's get this over with Agent, I hate looking at stiffs."

The sheriff followed the Special Agent into the tent and immediately regretted doing so with the smell that was inside. He almost gagged. The bodies themselves were all in different stages of decomposition and were far from being a pleasant sight. None of the faces that were still partially distinguishable were familiar to the sheriff, but he did recognize the clothing, and told the agent where they were from. He also told him that the group were very well armed, and if he wasn't careful, he'd have a full scale mini war on his hands.

Once the pond was cleared of all evidence, the special agent had the firemen refill the pond. They didn't see the point, but did so nevertheless. By the time the clean water had filled the pond to its previous level, it was much clearer than it had been before. As they had begun to fill it, the special agent had spoken to one of his agents before he drove away. He returned shortly after the fire crews had gone, and the bodies were being transported to the morgue.

The sheriff had also departed, he didn't feel well, so he never saw the FBI agents setting up their surveillance cameras around the lake. He also never saw them place cameras around the property of Charles Miller, and neither did Charles's security.

After what the sheriff had told him, Special Agent Martinez didn't want to start barging into the religious enclave asking questions. He didn't think he'd get anywhere doing that, so decided to build his case first by finding out who the victims were, and confirmation of how they actually died. He wanted to show patience, so he put a news block on the day's find, and hoped it would stick before he went and knocked on Charles Miller's door. But he got a huge break.

It was a couple of weeks later but a small dispute had gotten out of hand. One of the women had taken a young boy to her bed, when another woman, uninvited, had joined in. No one was supposed to do that, unless it was requested, but they were always welcome to watch, as indeed one other woman was doing. The uninvited woman was forgiven for joining in, but after doing it again just a few days later with the same woman and boy, a fight ensued. A very nasty fight.

After the two women were finally separated and treated for their cuts and bruises, a council was held when it was expected that the one who had joined in would apologize, and promise not to do so again unless it was with permission. For some reason she refused, almost causing another fight. Charles himself tried to reason with her. He'd slept with her several times and she had always been ready to please and had never been in any altercation. For some reason, she believed the young boy was hers to do with as she liked, and that the other woman knew that, yet was hogging the boy. Charles had to let her go.

The FBI had watched, but did nothing, when a vehicle headed into town and supplies were bought by the strange looking people, who looked like they'd be more at home on stage as a backing group. When Charles and his passenger left the compound and looked to be heading towards the lake, they moved quickly and quietly.

"Where are you taking me Charles?" She asked. "I thought you'd be dropping me off in town."

"Although you've been asked to leave, I have friends that we're going to meet up with, and I'm going to give you some money. My friends will take you wherever you want to go, and the cash will give you a fresh start."

"Are you scared of me telling tales Charles?"

"No, not at all. No one would believe you, you know that, and no one in the church would ever back up any story you came up with. I thought you were happy with us. Why did you make such a big thing of that boy?"

"He told me he loved me Charles," she explained. "No-one had ever said that to me before, and I love him. I didn't mind sharing him, but I just didn't want someone else having him alone. Now I've lost him completely. What's going to happen to me Charles?"

"You'll be okay. There's a place up ahead that I sometimes go to and just think about things. I think I'll take you there and we can talk some more and figure out what your next move is. Okay?"

"Yeah, that's okay. Is it far?"

"No, we're almost there."

As his agents moved closer, Special Agent Martinez was watching the television screens very intently, talking to everyone, and making sure they were keeping out of sight but as near as possible.

The car pulled up near the lake and they both got out. Charles walked the woman toward the pond, then pointed at a boulder that the FBI had found blood stains at, and the woman sat down. After watching Charles wander around as he talked to the woman, the agent saw him fumbling under the back of his shirt and commanded, "MOVE, MOVE, TAKE HIM DOWN!"

Charles was already pointing his gun at the back of the woman's head as the agents moved in, telling him loudly and very forcibly who they were and to drop his weapon, and he was so surprised that he actually did so. He'd always thought that if ever the authorities got on to him, he would go down firing, but here he was lying on his belly and facing God knew what. He was really mad with himself as he was read his rights, handcuffed, and put in the back of a car.

Special Agent Martinez was very happy. The gun that was retrieved was the same calibre as the weapon used on all the victims. The woman was safe and spilling her guts after realizing she had dodged death, and Reverend Charles Miller was in custody and facing multiple counts. He lawyered up, but the evidence was coming in that his gun was responsible for all the dead people in the lake, and was also now suspected of crimes against minors. Some of the dead had already been identified as child molesters, and now the Special Agent was ready to go to the compound. Without their leader, and they must have been wondering where he'd gotten to, he didn't think they would put up much resistance, and he had a warrant to search.

They pulled up at the compound gates in one car, like it was just a routine call. The two agents in the car got out of the car and acted very bored, like they were on a wild goose chase as the security detail came out of their gatehouse to see what they wanted. They should have stayed inside. Once they were outside, the agents served the warrant, disarmed them both, handcuffed them, and called in. By now they knew that the security detail was integral to the safety of the inhabitants of the compound, and with them out of the loop along with the Reverend, it was open to be secured by law enforcement. The FBI moved quickly before anyone could organize any kind of resistance, catching everyone off guard. Nobody fired a round.

They could barely believe what they found. Convicted sex offenders who were in violation of their parole and hadn't registered with the local cops. Children from the far east who could barely speak any English, but after being interviewed with interpreters, told their gruesome stories. Children of the followers who had also been violated. The altar that showed evidence of being used as a place of intercourse. The amount of arms that would have repelled a small army, and the food and water that would have ensured a very long and drawn out siege. There were also explosives that no one seemed to know anything about.

Reverend Charles Miller and his loyal followers were going to go down for a very long time, and most of them for life.

CHAPTER 35

It had been two years since Hannah had been introduced to the movie business, and she felt that life wasn't that bad. At first, she had been reluctant to comply with anything, but rather than beat her or rape her, they had given her space, and had her watch and learn. The older girls were really nice with her, telling her that the movies were all fake provided she listened to what she was told. They would even talk to her during scenes, when their faces were off camera and no dialogue was needed, which enforced their argument. Hannah learned that even when some guy had his huge penis inside her, she could almost ignore it, yet pretend she was experiencing pleasure.

So that was what she did. She faked everything so well that no-one could tell the difference, putting her mind elsewhere as all sorts of things were done to her. Hannah was only slowly developing which kept her in front of the cameras, but she was popular with the film crew, her co-stars, and the other girls. She was also getting perks now, and money was promised, as she performed in front of the cameras.

Generally, whatever the script, a rape was needed and Hannah was an excellent screamer and could cry on demand. Whoever the customers were, they couldn't get enough of Hannah and now she was teaching the new girls how to act.

Although she hadn't developed much physically, when she looked in the mirror she didn't see the same girl that had first arrived in the old building. Her eyes were colder, she looked more confident in herself, and she was nearly always in make up. Even when they wanted a girl au natural, she still wore make up. Her acne had gone, and her limp brown hair was now well cared for and full. She was also turning into a good looking young girl and had kept her tiny figure.

Hannah was friends now with Dee Romney, the woman who had lured her to this place. At first she had hated her, but over time, and after learning the ropes, she had gotten to like Dee who still worked in front of the camera. They had even been in the same movies, kissing and making out. Hannah thought that Dee was a great actress, she seemed real in their scenes together, and Hannah was now helping her sometimes with recruitment.

The child porn was proving to be far more lucrative than the teenage version, and the older girls were gradually leaving for other pastures. Hannah didn't know where they were going, but she was told they had been offered well paying movie roles with other film companies, so was happy for them, and thought the same thing would happen to herself when she got older. Little did she know.

When she went with Dee to meet girls, she came across as living proof of the success of the school. Hannah said all the right things, smiled a lot, looked happy, and dressed and appeared very well. If any of the girls had any doubt, they would look at Hannah and their discomfort would disappear. Dee travelled all over the place, and when she was able to take Hannah, it was greatly appreciated by her. Even when Dee booked a room and they shared a bed, Hannah didn't mind, as it was just another lesson that Dee was teaching her.

The new girls were always scared witless by their new surroundings and what was expected of them. Sometimes, force was needed after they failed to heed Hannah's instructions, and she was the first to condone it. Some of them would also ignore Hannah's teachings about the fake sex, and they would complain about the sperm being discharged. Hannah would tell them that the script demanded sperm, but that it was safe to swallow as the guys were all free of disease. Besides, they were thinking of their male partners when they finally came, certainly not the girls they were with. It was just movies.

They also did magazines which Hannah thought was easy. A lot of the time they would take stills from the movie, or Hannah would pose in various costumes and positions. She would even laugh sometimes as she was asked to stay perfectly still in a compromising position, or especially when she was given a mouthful of custard and she let it drool out of her mouth.

Apart from when she went with Dee, Hannah was still not allowed out alone but she wasn't bothered about it. She felt she had everything she needed. She was with her friends, and a recent perk, with a strict warning not to share it, had been the use of a computer with internet access. She loved going onto Facebook and twitter, making silly comments and being friended by total strangers. She could also watch movies on it and television shows she'd missed. Life wasn't bad anymore according to Hannah.

The movies and the magazines were big business, especially the movies that could be accessed online by a website's members, who paid well for the convenience. There were thousands of films, and the customers could type in their preferences to narrow their choices down. DVD's were also available, and they were made and shipped from a warehouse. All the labor in the factory was done by trafficked male and females who never left the warehouse. They worked day and night, received little food, and the most galling thing for them was that they had paid to get into the USA. At least their lot was better than most of the trafficked. They could just as easily have found themselves in the fields picking fruit or vegetables under the baking sun, or prostituted with up to twenty five johns a day. It all depended on their looks and ages. Families were broken apart and sent in different directions, and the youngest and the prettiest always got the worst of it. The house that Hannah was in had several Latinos, but there was a big demand for white kids which is were Dee came in. She only looked for Caucasian children, there were plenty of Latinos, as the most money was spent on the white kids.

The children that were being used for prostitution were all over the place. The website could also point the members to the different physical locations, and the members could also chat between themselves on the site. It was a very sophisticated operation and the website was very secure.

The operation was originally started by a Mexican gang member who had split away from his boss to go on his own. He'd survived a couple of attempts on his life by his old employer, but had retaliated after gaining members of his own. Finally, after a meeting, at which he swore he wasn't interested in trying to take over the drug operation of his former boss, he was left alone to pursue his own activities.

He went by the name of Jesus Hernandez, was only in his mid thirties, a wide and mean looking man, and he was legal in the USA. This gave him free reign to come and go over the border, which was really handy for him.

He had begun by smuggling, anyone who paid, over the border to start new lives. It then progressed into selling the illegals once they were in the US, and seeing the demand, especially for the smallest and the best looking, he started his own business selling them off. He called it Ideal Manpower, based it Arizona, and hired a very creative accountant to take care of the books. His business began to do well, and he didn't care one jot as to what happened to his countrymen. All he cared about was the welfare of his own family that he was just starting, and money. But he wanted more.

Recruiting more members to his gang, Jesus laid claim to a neighborhood by using his old boss's ruthless methods. Beheading his rivals and displaying them on the streets usually did the trick, and if it didn't, the bullets did. Very soon, no one wanted to mess with Jesus and his gang, and as he wasn't interested in the drug trade, his neighborhood was untouched. If anyone tried to sell their drugs on one of his corners, or in one of his buildings, they soon disappeared.

Jesus opened his own brothel, firstly with the good looking young women, then with the young ones. Jesus didn't like pedophiles at all, but they paid a lot of money on a constant basis, and as they spread the word around, there was no shortage of customers. After getting busted once, but not being there at the time, Jesus got careful. He started vetting the customers to find out who they really were, everyone was searched on entering the new brothel, and regular sweeps were done to look for bugs. Then he found William Butler. Although William always dressed down when he visited the brothel and only carried cash, Jesus discovered that William was a very wealthy man from being a hedge fund manager. William was also married with children, but a secret pedophile. He was exactly what Jesus had been looking for.

After very many conversations, William agreed to back Jesus with a very substantial investment, ideas, advice, and technology. William recouped his money within weeks, and the money kept rolling in. Jesus still kept his original brothel, but no longer seemingly had ties to it or any of the other parts of his empire. William had taken on people that were extremely knowledgable, recruiting from the website he had started for Jesus, and they had the website routed through so many countries it was almost impossible to follow. Every person that was hired was a sex offender, with skills to offer, and all the incentive in the world to keep everything secret.

Now, there was a brothel in very many cities, movies and magazines, international links, a regular supply of illegals from south of the border and some from the far east. There were also employees like Dee who would attract the white orphans, fostered, and runaway children.

Hannah thought she was doing well, was safe, and had a career in the movies. It didn't work like that, and she would eventually be taken away and sold on to a pimp in another part of the country. Or would be killed.

Jesus was making so much money he was having to invest it and put excess funds in overseas bank accounts. He had regular meetings with his 'generals' as he called them, and there was enough money to keep them extremely well paid.

William still lived a lie. On the surface, he was a highly successful man who not only had several homes, but also a very large yacht, a helicopter, jet, and a loving indulged family. He wasn't particularly handsome, but money had a way of making him seem desirable. Not liking the gym or jogging or anything, William was overweight, still retained a full head of dark hair, wore glasses, and wasn't prone to smiling a lot. His wife was very attractive, blonde and slim, and the children they had sired were also not short on looks. He was a father, but had always preferred sex with minors, and his daughter's friends always thought he looked at them weirdly.

William had never been arrested or even questioned. He'd read stories on the web that scared him to death, so he was always very careful about staying safe. He'd never been interested in buying or kidnapping his own child, but he would gladly pay big bucks for a virgin in a secure environment. He still paid, but now it was with a fake identity, and no one realized that he would get his money back tenfold.

To the astonishment of his wife, William was always being hit on by her divorced friends, which secretly flattered him. It was hard enough for him to get aroused by his wife, never mind her gold digging friends, but it was a constant source of amusement, and he would tell his wife if the woman was particularly annoying.

William still dreamt of the girl that had almost exposed him. She had been a friend of his daughter and had joined them on a cruise they took to the Caribbean. William adored her at first glance and the girl seemed to know it, and encouraged it. Whenever she looked in William's direction, she would lick her lips, or wink at him. When she sunbathed in her tiny bikinis, she would pose seductively, and if no one was looking she would also touch herself. William thought she was a Lolita, but he couldn't take his eyes off her, and when she whispered in his ear one day that she wanted him to take her virginity, he almost succumbed. Instead, he took out his frustration on his wife who thought it was the best cruise ever, even though she never knew her husband was thinking of the girl the whole time. When the girl realized she wasn't going to get the head man, she diverted her attention to William's son, who wasn't as strong willed as his father, and William still ended up having to pay her a hefty sum to stay quiet.

The girl was a mother now and married to a guy in William's circle. Whenever he saw her, she would still wink, and the way other men looked at her, he knew she was unfaithful. She was just too old now for William.

William loved his life. He sometimes wondered what his reaction would have been if a man like himself had ever taken his daughter at a very young age, and he always thought he would have gone crazy and killed him. But he never thought he was like that. William had come from a family that was very comfortable, and it had always been instilled in him that they had earned it, and that everyone was capable of being as financially secure. That he had earned multiple times the money than his family had only reinforced that belief, so he was very disdainful of the poor. He never thought for one moment that life could be bad for people. It was their own fault they were poor and he never had any sympathy for them. The girls he paid for was just an extension of that opinion, and they deserved the treatment they got.

His wife would often want to donate money to different organizations, but the only ones he had sympathy toward were the animal charities. Again, he blamed the poor for their own plight, but the animals couldn't determine their own future so he donated money to help. What he would really liked to have donated to was the extermination of the people who abused the animals, or hunted them out of existence.

Instead, his money went to shelters and organizations designed to keep them safe and well.

Compared to William, Jesus was a well-adjusted and regular guy. To Jesus, a pedophile was the worst of the worst even though they were filling his pockets. When he had consulted with William, most of the time he had wanted to wring the life out of his smug and unsmiling face, and had since tried to avoid any face to face meetings with him. Jesus wasn't disdainful of the poor people he preyed on, he thought there was just too many due to breeding too much. He also thought they were weak. If he had ever found himself in a situation where he was working for nothing, or had to let another man screw him, he would have fought and died if necessary. Out of all the people he had transported over the border, or had sold, the only ones he had respect for were the ones who had resisted. That he'd killed them, or had them killed by others was of no consequence to him. At least they had tried. The ones he made money from had no resistance, so he never gave them a thought.

One of the boys that had been taken to Hannah's house was called Javier and Hannah was getting to like him. He'd listened to her advice, did as he was told, and didn't ask awkward questions. He also spoke good English, and although Hannah had learned a lot of Spanish and could get by, she still preferred talking in her own language.

Out of curiosity, Hannah had asked Javier where he'd come from, and after he told her the name of a tiny village in the middle of Mexico, she had looked it up on the google map. Days later, she asked him if he had any family and he said he had a mother and father along with an older sister. More days passed and then Hannah asked him if his family were still at home in Mexico. He replied that he didn't know where they were.

Hannah didn't speak to him again until she returned from a trip with Dee. She was beginning to think that Dee was getting way more enjoyment from her sex lessons than she admitted to, her moans were just too realistic to Hannah's ears. It began to dawn on Hannah that Dee was using her for her own pleasure. It didn't hinder the job in hand. They had brought back a very pretty girl who was all excited, and Hannah began to advise the girl once she realized what she had got into.

When Hannah spoke again to Javier, she asked more than the usual one question, and she learned that he and his family were very poor, but had gotten together enough money to pay for a way into the USA. They had family members in California, and if they could make their way to them, they had work and money to look forward to. However, on crossing the border, they had been split up at gun point, and Javier had seen his family depart in different directions before he was brought to this place, along with a couple of girls who had also been taken from their families. When he had asked where his family had been taken to, he was hit on the head by the butt of a gun, and told to stay quiet and mind his own business. If he didn't, he and his family would all be killed.

This worried Hannah and out of curiosity, she looked up the pretty girl who had just arrived and the town news. It was the top story. It was being reported as a kidnap and her parents were pleading for answers and communication. The mother was saying that she'd had a disagreement with her daughter on the morning of her disappearance, but it was nothing serious. She also said that since they had adopted her, they felt their family was complete, and now it was shattered. If anyone knew of her whereabouts then to please call the number below, which was anonymous so that they didn't need to get involved. Hannah decided she needed to talk to the girl, to see if any of this was true, or if the mother was just spinning stories for the media.

The girl was called Alice, a blonde curly haired girl with dimples on both cheeks. By the time Hannah had chance to speak to her, she'd already been put into one movie, and the happy face that Hannah remembered was now replaced with a serious glum look.

"Hey Alice, it's me Hannah". The look that Hannah was given was one that she expected. It was full of distrust and she tried to ignore Hannah.

"Alice, I just need to ask you something. What was so wrong with your home that you wanted to leave? Weren't you being abused?"

Alice wondered whether to reply. She thought Hannah was really nice when she'd met her and Dee, but it was all a lie, and now she was trapped in this hell hole, making porn movies.

"My adopted mom wouldn't let me go to a sleep over that I was invited to. She said she didn't trust my friend who was having it, as she was sure she would invite boys as well."

"Do you think she would have had boys there?" Asked Hannah.

"Probably. But nothing would have happened, it would have been fun. She's always telling me what I can and can't do, like she knows better than me."

"So that was the only reason you wanted to leave, because of the sleep over?"

"Yes. How many times do I have to tell you. I was being mistreated." Alice answered with annoyance.

"Okay, just wondered is all. I won't ask you anything else."

Hannah left her be, and decided to ask some of the others how they had gotten here. She wasn't asking openly, just when she could speak quietly as she didn't want to arouse any suspicion from the adults. She didn't like what she heard. She had thought all the kids were like herself, in a home where she didn't belong, and was being abused. Physically or sexually. Running away was always an option, and she felt sure that she herself would have done so again, eventually.

But most of the other kids had been wrenched from their families forcibly and now had no idea where they were. That wasn't right and Hannah wondered what to do about it to help, but she sure as hell didn't want to go back to her home. Although, after looking on the internet, they had made a big fuss of her going, and the police were still looking for her even after all this time. That was a big surprise to Hannah, as was her adopted parents saying they really missed her, had mistakenly used corporal punishment to keep the children in line, and now wanted forgiveness.

Although Hannah had a computer and internet access, she had to hand it over every night, presumably so that someone could check on what she'd been looking at and which sites. So if she created an email address or used her old one, it would show up on the laptop. She could tweet or send a message on Facebook, but even those could be looked at. She'd been careful with the news sites she'd gone to, erasing them from the history then filling the history with other sites like YouTube and MTV. Leaving messages though was really risky, and she decided she would have to use Dee's phone.

Dee had gone away again and it was a few days before Hannah saw her in the house again. She watched Hannah do a scene with another girl, and when the shout of "That's a wrap," went up, Dee walked up to the set, which was just a couch, and said hello to Hannah, who was putting on her robe.

"Hi Dee, how are you? I haven't seen you for a while."

"I had to go pick up someone. She's downstairs being shown the ropes. I missed having you on the trip Hannah, but I enjoyed the scene you just did."

"Thank you. Say Dee, are you here for a while?"

"I think so, why do you ask?"

Hannah moved toward her, close, so that she wouldn't be overheard by the crew.

"I was wondering if I could come to your room tonight."

Dee could smell Hannah's scent and the other girl's quite clearly now.

"Do you need another lesson Hannah?"

"No. I was thinking of real sex without the faking. I've been thinking of you and your body and I want you Dee. Is that bad of me?"

Dee wanted to kiss her right there and then. Although it had always been 'lessons' previously, Dee had never held back, but knew that Hannah had, and now here she was, wanting real sex with her.

"Come over after dinner. I'll be waiting for you."

Dee walked away, happy as could be, wanting to prepare herself for what she thought was going to be Hannah's coming out party, and she had been chosen as the special one.

As Hannah took her shower, she knew she would have to let herself go, if only a little, to convince Dee. She had acted like a machine for so long now she didn't know if she preferred boys or girls. The main thing she didn't like was the rough skin on the men chafing her skin. She just needed that cell phone for a couple of minutes when Dee went to sleep, and the phone number to call about Alice.

Hannah had another couple of scenes to do later with men, so after her shower she had a bite to eat and got the laptop. Thankfully, the number was still on the home page of the newspaper, so if her history was checked, then it would appear that she was just looking at the local news, which was now about the basketball team and a very short blurb about Alice with the telephone number, but no picture. It was a simple number and Hannah could easily remember it.

She also knew now where exactly the house was after coming and going a few times.

The scenes went fairly well with the men, there were a few cuts, but that was normal as the director wanted some things done differently before he was satisfied. Hannah had seen Alice in the studio next to her during one of the cuts, and she was pretending to fight someone off, screaming, as her clothing was gradually torn off her. Hannah had done many similar scenes, not thinking about them, but as she watched Alice she realized how young Alice was, and how young she was when she first had to do it. Hannah was grateful when she was called back to her own set. The man who had been doing the fake rape on Alice, was now about to enter her.

Knocking on Dee's door after dinner, Hannah wasn't surprised to find her in a buttoned up blouse that showed her lace bra beneath, a pencil skirt, stockings and knee high boots. Dee liked to be undressed as slowly as possible from sexy clothing. Hannah herself had dressed for Dee, and Dee liked her being naked beneath a flowery summery dress, with buttons at the front.

"I think this deserves a drink Hannah," she commented, after taking her tongue out of Hannah's mouth once they were inside. Hannah had felt the intensity of Dee as they kissed. "Let me introduce you to champagne."

Dee went to her fridge and retrieved a bottle, opening the drink with a loud pop as the cork flew to the other side of the room. Two glasses were already waiting, and she poured slowly before putting the bottle down, took the two glasses and handed one to

Hannah. "Welcome to the first night of your life," she toasted. They clinked their glasses and took a sip. Hannah liked it.

It was over three hours before Dee finally fell asleep, and Hannah really wanted to as well, but instead, got off the bed, found Dee's phone in her purse and took it into the bathroom. She dialed the numbers as she sat on the toilet, and leaned over to turn the faucet on in the sink. She didn't wait to be asked any questions once it was established it was the anonymous hotline to the missing Alice. Instead, she told the officer where she was, what she was doing, and that there were other children as well. Then she hung up, flushed the toilet, washed her hands, fixed her face and hair, then went back to the bedroom. Just as she put the phone back, Dee turned onto her back and raised herself onto her elbows.

"Are you going back to your own room lover?" She asked, still sleepy.

"No, I'm thirsty. I was just getting another glass of champagne," replied Hannah, from what was the second bottle.

"Then come back to bed. I want to cuddle with you."

"I was actually wondering," teased Hannah as she stood next to the bed. "What would you taste like in champagne."

Dee opened her eyes and gave her a sly smile. This had been her best night ever, and despite her exhaustion, didn't want it to end.

"Then why don't you find out lover, but don't use it all. I'd like to return the favor."

Hannah was still in deep sleep when she felt Dee shaking her awake. "Come on Hannah, wake up. You can't be found in here naked. We have to move!"

"Oh please Dee, let me sleep a bit longer, it's not even light yet," Hannah pleaded, turning over in the bed.

"Hannah, the cops are here asking questions. You have to move. NOW."

Hearing the word cops got Hannah moving. She never thought they would be this quick. She jumped out of bed and threw on her dress before heading for the door. Dee stopped her before she left.

"If they find you Hannah, you're eighteen and want to be here. Go to the back of the house and we'll hide you and the others until the cops leave. If they do find you, tell them what I told you. Now run."

Hannah ran to her own room first, quickly changing into underwear, jeans and tee shirt, before heading to the back of the house. A couple of security guys were counting everyone as they arrived, and when they had the number they wanted, they moved the kids down into the basement and told them to stay quiet, as they closed and locked the door on them.

All the kids were wondering what was going on above them, as they heard running and shouting, and then a couple of shots were fired and then more yelling. Originally, only two cops had arrived. There had been many false leads, so Hannah's call was responded to, but not with any great urgency or manpower. If it hadn't been for the security guard at the gate pulling his gun, then they would probably have just turned around. Luckily, he wasn't able to get a shot off before they disarmed him, but that set the alarm bells ringing and the two cops had to wait at the gatehouse until a warrant was issued, and the cavalry arrived.

After making sure that the exterior was secure, they moved in. They caught the occupants unawares as it was so early in the morning. After getting all the adults together in a first level room, it was then discovered that the cellar was locked, and with no one volunteering a key, they broke open the door. After finding all the children, which came after seeing the movie sets, they had already guessed what was being done to them before even seeing the recordings. Best of all, they also had the computers before they'd been wiped or destroyed.

As soon as the children were found, child services were notified and they were kept in a separate room from the adults, who were all being arrested and cuffed. It was a huge bust and soon the FBI had taken over, poring over everything, especially the computers, and cataloging evidence from everywhere.

The adults were all taken away in paddy wagons, and child services were slowly moving the children. Alice was one of the first to leave and was already in hospital, being examined, processed and interviewed with her very happy parents in attendance. As Hannah was one of the older girls, she was one of the last to leave, and once in hospital she too was processed and examined, and then interviewed.

Because she had never had time to shower after being with Dee, she had her DNA all over her as well as champagne. Hannah was told she had someone else's body fluids mixed with her own, so it was only a matter of time before they found out who.

Surprisingly to Hannah, she had liked being with Dee and liked how she had made her feel. She didn't know what to do or say. They would also soon know who she was from her picture, fingerprints and DNA, but she still wasn't sure about going back to her new parents.

It was pointed out to Hannah that all the adults who'd had sex with her would be charged with rape of a minor, and that they were all going to jail for a long time. Even the film crews and the security personnel. They told her there was nothing else to fear, and that after therapy and guidance, she would get her old life back. Finally, realizing that she didn't have to make any more movies or pose for magazines, and that Dee would have to go to prison, she began to talk. How she had been taken to the house and by who, what she had to do, how she helped to take others there, and her fears about going home.

It was decided, after time, that it was best for Hannah not to return to her home and to make a fresh start elsewhere, which she did, and was very happy there. She was never interested in boys ever again.

Eventually, after following a myriad of false avenues, the FBI found where the money was going after they'd traced all the customers. Hundreds of pedophiles were arrested and convicted of possessing child porn, amongst other charges.

William Butler and Jesus Hernandez were also arrested. Almost as soon as Jesus had his cuffs put on, one of his 'general's' had taken over his business, and apart from the movies, it was seamless. There were plenty of buyers for the illegals, and as soon as they safely arrived in the US, they were shipped off. Javier's parents and sister were never found, but he was allowed to go to his relatives in San Diego.

William, who had never thought he would be arrested for anything, was devastated and forever ashamed as he rotted away in his cell. He was surrounded by poor people who wanted to hurt him, and totally abandoned by his family and friends.

CHAPTER 36

Olivia Danville, the agent in San Francisco, strongly suspected that another child brothel had opened in the city. There were also rumors of trafficked children in private homes, from Oakland to Sacramento, and a tip about slave farm workers south of Stockton. She felt like she'd never been busier.

At home, her husband Kyle was an absolute rock. She didn't know what she would do without him as he took care of everything in and around the home. Olivia missed her girls like crazy. Especially the small things like taking them to school, picking them up, taking them to their various after school activities. Sometimes she would get home in time to go with them, but mostly it fell to Kyle to do it, and she missed them. Normally, Olivia had the weekends free unless a case was about to close, so the family would go to the beach, or to a movie, or just hang out together at home.

The girls, Jemima and Chelsea were now nine and seven respectively. Like their mother, they were dark haired and small, but way cuter than Mom. As she was working so much, they could also twist her round their little fingers. Kyle would complain if Olivia gave in to one of their demands, when he had emphatically said no, but as the girls had Olivia in the palm of their hands, she had Kyle. He was like putty sometimes, and Olivia wondered how on earth she deserved him.

It was difficult for Olivia, with her work, not to be over protective of the girls, but Kyle kept her in the loop by texting her throughout the day, with messages like 'arrived at school', 'picked up from school', 'soccer practice starting', 'swim lessons now', 'no-one drowned', 'home safe'. Olivia would send back her own messages, 'be home on time', 'don't make me dinner', 'need a drink', 'kiss the girls', 'wanting you'.

During the week, it was much easier for Olivia as the girls were going to school as she went to work, but if she was called out at weekend, they would beg her not to go. The last time it happened they said they would forgive her if they got a puppy. Olivia had agreed but had yet to break the news to Kyle, who would be the chief caregiver and trainer. They would also need to decide what kind of dog, which was why she had deferred the decision. The two girls couldn't agree on the type, and if Kyle agreed, his choice would be completely different. There was also a vacation to think about. Olivia always took her vacation time. It was important as it gave her chance to completely relax and unwind. Not to mention the time she got with the girls, playing, and just having fun.

The department had just closed a very old case. A girl had gone missing from the Santa Cruz boardwalk over ten years ago. It was in broad daylight with thousands of people around, yet no one had see a thing. At least nothing that had led to anything. Thousands of photos had been gone through from tourists cameras and phones, yet nothing had surfaced.

Years later, a car was stopped for speeding, and the driver was a convicted sex offender who had a young woman and two children in his car. The cop was suspicious, even though the young woman said she was a niece of the man. Although he just gave the driver a ticket and let him go, he asked questions once he was back at the station.

Over the phone, the parole officer said the man had no relatives apart from his wife, who still lived with him. The woman and the kids were probably his wife's relatives, as she had a couple of brothers. The parole officer thought he'd seen a photo or two in the house of a young woman and her two children, but they were certainly not living there.

"So you don't know who these kids are exactly, or where they live?" Asked the policeman.

"No idea. But I do know they are not staying with the perp, as I checked out his house just last week and there were no signs of any children."

After finishing his call, the cop was still unhappy, so once he finished his shift he staked out the house. Nothing happened. It seemed like a complete waste of time. He couldn't start barging his way inside, so he went home to his wife, who was curious as to why he couldn't let go of this guy.

"I don't know," he explained. "He just seemed too smug. And the look on the mother was scared, even though she said she was his niece. It just didn't seem right."

"You have a gut feeling about this don't you?"

"I do. I just know something is very wrong."

"Then you need to follow it through. If it comes to nothing then no harm is done, but if something is going on, then you'll never forgive yourself."

The cop knew he had no grounds for getting a search warrant, and a detective confirmed it for him. But the detective did tell him to keep his eye open for the young woman, and if she was ever alone to just have a quiet word with her. In the meantime, he could watch the house, and if the woman and the two kids were living there, then he could grab the parole officer and march him down there. The perp was not allowed to have children living in the house, even if they were relatives.

So he watched whenever he could, but the woman never stepped out of the house without the perp or his wife. But she and her kids did appear to be living there, so he went to see the parole officer.

He didn't like the parole officer. As soon as he stepped into his office, the PO was complaining about the amount of cases he had, and not having enough time to devote to any of them. The PO was adamant that no children were living in the property. There were no signs of anything to indicate any children had even been in there.

"No toys lying around?" Asked the cop.

"Nothing, and I don't have time to keep going over to somebody's house just on someone's whim. I'm already overworked."

"Look. I've been staking that house out on my own time and I'm telling you that kids are living in there.

Are you going to go over there or do I have to go over your head?" Asked the annoyed cop.

"Okay, okay. I'll go over in the morning. Does that satisfy you!"

"What time are you going? I want to meet you there."

"There's no point in doing that. I'll let you know what I find, which will be nothing, just as it always is."

"What time will you be there?" Said the cop through gritted teeth.

"If you insist, I'll be there at 9am. Then we can waste both our times."

The cop hurried out before he slapped him, and was waiting at the house the following day when the PO arrived.

"Well, we at least know they're home," greeted the PO.

"You called to say we were coming?" Asked the appalled cop.

"Of course I did. It's bad enough coming to the other side of town but it's even worse when no one is home."

The cop was seething as they were let inside the home and found absolutely nothing, apart from some pictures of the husband and wife with the young woman and her two children.

"See. I told you there was nothing. Now can we go?"

"Is there a cellar?"

"No. This is it. Have you had enough now?"

"What's out back?"

The PO walked the cop to the rear window of the family room.

"You see? Just a yard and some trees."

"Why is there a barbed wire fence around the trees?"

"They said they were having problems with intruders, which are a real problem around here. There's a lot of burglaries in this part of town."

"Have you ever taken a look?"

"Had no need to officer, its just grass and trees out there."

The officer went to the rear door and stepped outside, and noticed that apart from the barbed wire, the fence around the yard was very high. As he got closer to the trees he noticed there was a low building behind, covered in camouflage, and then a gate at the rear of the wire fence that could only open from the one side. Beyond it, there were some toys scattered around. Letting himself in, he was already cursing before he even opened the door to the poorly constructed one room outbuilding, and he couldn't help but exclaim, "Oh my fucking God!"

He stayed there as he made a call and waited for help. Looking around, it was plainly obvious that the young woman and her two children lived here. There was just one bed that looked like it had come from a dump, cardboard boxes that contained clothing, a bowl with water in that they probably washed in, toothbrushes and toothpaste, a small camping toilet, a camping stove, and some cans of food with a dirty saucepan. The three occupants were huddled together in a corner, scared of what this cop would do to them, not realizing he was here saving them.

Because of the high risk call he had placed, the cop didn't have to wait long for reinforcements to arrive. As soon as they realized what was going on, they called in the FBI, and they arrested the perp and his wife, while the PO was too ashamed to speak about his ignorance.

The young woman knew who she was, and was indeed the girl who had gone missing in Santa Cruz. She said both the man and the woman had taken her, saying they knew where her parents were after she'd wandered off looking for some cotton floss. They had bought her some, but then bundled her into the trunk of their car and drove away. Since then, she had lived here. The man had fathered her two children and the woman had helped with the births. The woman hadn't seemed to mind her husband raping her and making her pregnant, and the reason she had never tried to runaway was firstly because she would never have been able to do so with the kids, and secondly, because the man repeatedly threatened to kill them, after he raped them. She was just so scared of what he would do to the kids, that she just couldn't leave them for him to do as he pleased with them. She was also worried about what her parents would think. She'd been naughty on the boardwalk and had walked away from her parents, and now she had children because she hadn't been strong enough to fight back.

She needn't have worried. Her parents feared the worst when the agent knocked on their door and asked them to sit down once inside their house. Then they were leaping and crying for joy, even after the agent told them what had happened to her during the past ten years.

No one could believe that a registered sex offender, who under no circumstances was to be allowed access to children at all, had a parole officer who repeatedly ignored the rules because he was too busy. Needless to say, he was fired, and the cop was promoted and given a recommendation.

The young woman and her children eventually went home to her delighted and very happy parents, while the perp and his wife pleaded guilty to all the charges against them, and the perp forsook his parental rights.

CHAPTER 37

An undercover agent was trying to find and get into the child brothel, but so far with no success. He'd found a couple of regular ones, but nobody seemed to be talking about the child brothel, neither the hookers or the pimps. He'd been looking for one pimp in particular who owed him a favor, but he seemed to have gone deep underground. Even his women hadn't seen him.

Then he saw him one day walking down California Street toward the business section of San Francisco. He'd had work done on his features.

"Hey, Dwight," he greeted him, "I'd never have recognized you without those God awful clothes you wear. What's happened to your face man? You look almost handsome."

Dwight's favorite color was purple and as usual he was covered in it, along with his usual fedora. Most pimps tried to blend in with everyone else, but not Dwight, he was old school.

"Hey, Agent Deeks. You like my new look? Got my nose and my teeth fixed, and them old bags under my eyes have gone. Looks good huh?"

Dwight had been beaten up really badly several years previously, and had never regained his looks.

"Looks good Dwight," said the agent inspecting his face. "You got a good surgeon."

"I wasn't going to one of these backstreet goons. Besides, the surgeon has a certain taste so we did a deal. So you need a girl Agent?"

Dwight had been the Agent's informer for years. Dwight had no time for drug dealers or gangs, so he'd given Deeks a lot of information over the years, and as he kept his girls healthy as well, Deeks looked after him.

Deeks was a single guy, fairly handsome, with short blonde hair, a worked out body, and a face that offended nobody. As usual, he was in jeans and tee shirt, a sport jacket hiding his gun and keeping out of the chill of the city.

"No, I don't need a girl Dwight. I need to know the location of the child brothel."

"Well If I'd known you were into kids I would never have befriended you man," Dwight joked. "But you need to stay away from those bad folk. They're even meaner since the last time you busted them."

"They're the same people?"

"Same people putting up the money and smuggling the kids, just different faces."

"Do you know where they're operating from?"

"No, I have no idea. Not in my neighborhood, but I know of another pimp who deals with them."

"How would I get an invite?"

"I could pass the word that some white guy is looking to hook up with a small Chinese girl, but I heard they need proof these days that their customers like kids."

"What kind of proof Dwight?"

"A picture or a movie is what I heard."

"If I can come up with something like that, what will happen next?"

"I give you the name and location of the pimp who you will approach and show him the evidence. Then he'll have you meet him somewhere where he'll search you, then take you to the house with your head covered. I'll give you his name now if you repay the favor."

"What's the favor Dwight?"

"One of my girls got herself arrested last night soliciting an undercover cop. I hate these undercover cops," Dwight smiled.

"Okay, I'll see to it. Now who is this pimp?"

"He calls himself Mr. Chan and he hangs out in Chinatown on Stockton Street. He moves up and down but you can't miss him. He's always dressed in black pants and a Hawaiian shirt. If it's cold he wears a turtle neck below the shirt. The guy has no style."

Deeks thought that was funny coming from Dwight.

"Your girl is in the usual station?"

"Yeah. She calls herself Bonnie, but she isn't bonnie!"

"Okay Dwight, I'll see you later."

"I can still get you a girl, on the house."

"You'd probably send me Bonnie. Not this time Dwight. Stay safe man."

"You too agent. I can recommend a surgeon to you when you eventually look in a mirror and see how ugly you are."

Deeks laughed as he walked away, taking a glance at his reflection in a store window to make sure he hadn't lost his looks.

Olivia wasn't too enamored with the plan, especially the photo or movie. There was no way they could have a young girl be photographed with an agent in a compromising position. They would all be looking for another job. Then someone suggested photoshopping. If they could find a movie or a photo of one of the kids they'd found, maybe the kid would agree to her image being used, with the agent's face replacing the john. Then if it came up in evidence, they would be able to prove the picture was photoshopped. It was a good idea.

Olivia had the agent look through the evidence files and boxes to find a suitable photo, with a girl they still kept in touch with, and would maybe want to help bust an operation.

Ashley was doing very well these days, and her home tutor was very impressed with how well she was doing, and her intelligence. All the remnants of the drugs had gone from her face. It was now full instead of gaunt, her teeth had been fixed, the scars from injections had almost disappeared, and she was no longer painfully thin. She was a very attractive woman. She was no longer in touch with Sandy. Sandy's family had moved away almost as soon as they got her home, and Ashley had never tried to find her.

When Olivia knocked on her door, she received a very warm welcome as she always did. The last time they had spoken, Ashley had said she wanted to become an agent herself one day, as soon as she got the necessary qualifications to apply. She sometimes sent an email to Olivia, saying she was still intent on doing that. Because Olivia's visit could stir up bad memories, Olivia had called Ashley's parents to ask them to be there when she came round, as she was going to ask something that may be difficult.

Once they were all sitting down and enjoying a coffee, Olivia told them how they were trying to take down another child brothel, and that the only way they could get in was having an undercover agent get an invitation. There were photos of Ashley that they'd found in the Las Vegas house, with different customers, that were presumably taken for leverage against the customers. Olivia asked if they could use some of the photos, and superimpose their agent in place of the customer, as that was what they needed to get him inside the house.

This was a bolt from the blue about the photos. They had never been told before of their existence, and they all wanted to know how many there were, and where they were.

Olivia explained that they were found well into Ashley's recovery, and Olivia herself didn't want to tell her about them in case it affected her recovery in any way. The photos were not public, but they had helped to locate several pedophiles, and they were locked away in a secure evidence vault.

Ashley had no hesitation in saying yes, but her parents needed more reassurances. That Ashley wouldn't have to do any posing, or give evidence, and if the photos could be destroyed. Olivia promised they would be destroyed, even doing it personally if need be. No posing or giving evidence would be required.

She had her photos for the undercover agent, and if Ashley ever applied to join the FBI, Olivia was going to support her application and help her to get in.

Deeks hated the photos, they almost made him sick. Even though he'd been placed into the photos, they looked so real, and he prayed that his friends and family would never see them. They would never have spoken to him again.

Putting them inside his jacket pocket, and trying to look as slimy as he could, he went to Stockton Street to find Mr. Chan. Just as Dwight had said, he was easy to find.

"Mr. Chan?" Deeks asked of the man standing alone in a doorway. "Are you Mr. Chan?"

Chan looked him over with boredom on his face.

"Who wants to know? Are you a cop?"

"No, I'm not a cop. You can search me if you want," replied Deeks, who kept looking around suspiciously.

"Is someone watching you Mr?"

"No, but someone might be watching you."

"No one is watching me Mr. Why do you think they are?"

"Because I was told you can get me what I need Mr. Chan."

"And what might that be?"

Deeks again looked around, and his voice going even lower said, "I need a young girl Mr. Chan."

It was Chan's turn to look around, and seeing no one suspicious asked, "Who told you about me?"

Deeks gave him the name of a pimp who Chan would know of, but not be a close friend to.

"Did he tell you the cost and what you need to prove?"

"He didn't tell me the price but he told me about the proof."

"Step into the doorway Mr., while I frisk you down."

Finding no gun, no wire, or badge, he told Deeks to show him the proof.

Deeks showed him a photo from his wallet, that Chan looked disgusted by.

"What age you want Mr? Boy or girl?"

"Around ten. A girl, and she's got to be pretty."

"They're all pretty Mr. A virgin will cost you five thousand for an hour, otherwise a thousand. These girls are good Mr., guaranteed to give you the most pleasure you've ever had. If you want more hours, or all night, then we can deal."

"Two hours with a non virgin will suit me. Can you arrange it?"

"You want Asian, or Mexican? If you want a White girl then it's more money and a longer wait."

"Asian," replied Deeks.

"When do you want to do this?"

"This week. Anytime will do."

"Be here tomorrow, the same time. with the money. Now go Mr."

Deeks left and made sure he wasn't followed before going back to the office.

"We're on for tomorrow Boss," he told Olivia. "Same time, same place."

"Did he frisk you?"

"Yes."

"I think we have to expect an electronic shake down tomorrow. We'll have to follow you. I think I have an idea that will work. Okay, good, I'll get everyone organized."

San Francisco has a lot of cyclists and skate boarders, and after asking many agents and other agencies if they had people who could skateboard or cycle the hills in San Francisco, she got a team together.

As Deeks met Mr. Chan and handed over the marked money before getting into a car and being hooded, a skateboarder swooped by and planted a homing device beneath the car, followed by another skateboarder who did the same thing in case one fell off. The cyclists then took turns following, along with a few cars who kept a very safe distance away. The car pulled into a large garage on Taylor Street, and twenty minutes later, the house was broken into from the front, the back, and the roof.

Deeks had been taken to a room containing a tiny Chinese girl who immediately started to try to undress him. She was dressed in the tiniest of skirts and top, and was really pretty. Deeks wondered how she had gotten here. If she'd been sold by poor parents or just taken while she played. He pointed to the bathroom and then himself to say he needed to use it, and as he washed his hands, he wondered how he could stall before the noise of the bust forced him into action. As he didn't have a weapon, his instructions had been to secure the room once it went down, then to wait for a knock on the door. He went back into the bedroom where the girl was lying seductively on the bed, and indicated for her to take a shower. She smiled at his motions, and happily went into the bathroom, taking her clothes off quite brazenly in front of him.

"Oh fuck," he whispered to no one. "Please hurry."

He'd noticed the cameras in the room and bathroom, and the girl was calling and signaling for him to join her, but instead he sat down and pretended to watch her, as she soaped herself like a porn star.

Then he heard the noise from below and thanking his own guardian angel, he grabbed the chair and wedged it under the door handle. He then manhandled a chest of drawers over to the door to reinforce the chair. Then he went to the bathroom, indicated to her to get dressed, threw her a robe, and waited for someone to knock.

It seemed to last forever and Deeks felt very frustrated that he was unarmed and couldn't go and help his colleagues, who he heard firing rounds as they were shot at.

Someone barged the door but the chair and chest held firm, and whoever had tried to get in, left without trying again.

Not too long after, there was a knock on the door. It was Olivia, and he moved the chest and the chair away to let her in.

It was a good bust. No agents were killed or any of the other law enforcement personnel, but six of the traffickers died of their wounds. Mr. Chan was arrested.

CHAPTER 38

The tip about the farm workers, or slaves more like, was made by a former, paid picker of the farm, who then had to scramble to find another job. He'd been going to that particular farm for years, working the fields as an itinerant. It was a family business for him and they relied on it. Many other families did as well. The children and the partners helped to pick, to get the bonuses that were offered, which afforded a nest egg for the lean times.

It was a tight community as a picker. Gossip quickly spread, and if one farm was offering better rates and conditions than another, it created a bargaining chip for them. They didn't like changing farms, they stayed very loyal if they were treated well and were paid the going rate. So when they arrived at the farm at the usual date, it was a huge shock to them to discover they weren't needed anymore, other arrangements had been made, and they were free to find work elsewhere.

They did so, and soon the regular picking crew were together again at another nearby farm, that had always had trouble finding regular pickers because they paid less. Not much, but enough to make a difference.

Most of the pickers were illegal immigrants who only came into the US for the picking season, following the hot sun as it ripened the produce. Once done, they headed home, with money in their pockets that was eventually spread around the tiny villages they lived in. It's a hard life picking, not many want to do it, and if it wasn't for the illegals, most of the produce wouldn't get sold and the prices would soar.

They knew the farmer that dismissed them was a cheapskate, as he always complained about everything. He would moan about having to pay the going rate, the pickers speed, or that half of the harvest was rotten. He'd always been that way, they'd gotten used to it, but they never expected to be let go.

Everybody wondered who had replaced them, and it must have been for much less pay. Which didn't make sense. They decided to have someone go back and take a look at who was doing the picking, and to see if they could find out anything else.

Ramone was chosen and he decided to go on a Sunday. Partly because it was the day off, and partly because then he could ask the pickers how much they were being paid. If he could find them of course.

It was only about an hour from his new farm to the old one, and after he parked his truck to go and take a look at the fields that were set way back off the road, he was shocked to find they were picking. He was even more shocked to see men seated in high chairs, covered by umbrellas to keep them in the shade, as if they were umpires at a tennis match. The field that was being picked was being done so by a huge amount of people, children included, all bent double as they dug in the earth. He looked again at the men watching, and he saw they all had rifles and radios.

Ramone wondered what on earth was going on, so he decided to stay after going back to his truck for some food and water, then found a shady spot where he wouldn't be seen. They picked until dusk when a whistle was blown, and Ramone felt for them as they emptied their baskets and walked slowly, hunched over from bending so long, in the same direction. The men from the chairs had now joined the pickers, and they walked on the outside, waving their rifles, and Ramone heard them telling the pickers to hurry up.

Ramone followed them at a safe distance, watching as they approached a barn that was used to store the picked produce until it was picked up the following morning. Outside the barn, a long table had been set up, and to Ramone it looked like a food station, with large pans on burners, trays, and two people, older people, manning it. As the pickers approached, they formed a line, and as they walked by the table were handed paper plates with what looked like to Ramone, tortillas on them. They were each given two, and then they took a cup and dipped it into a huge bowl, which he thought must be water. Most of the pickers sat down on the dirt to eat and drink, then when they'd finished, they took their cup and plate to a large garbage container and threw them in. No one asked for, or had gotten more water or food, and after dumping their rubbish, they all went into the barn. Once everybody was inside, including the two cooks after they cleared up, the men from the chairs locked them all in and departed.

Ramone left, and when he returned to his family and friends, he was surprised they were waiting for him, as it was dark now and they had a long day's work tomorrow. He told them what he'd seen and everybody tried to guess what was going on. One man, an older member, said he'd heard stories before that were similar, and that it could be the only answer. They were working as slaves.

Nobody could believe that, and arguments erupted about it. After the talk died down, the old man said he had come across a man, who after entering the country, had been taken to a farm at gun point along with many others, and had been forced to work from dawn to dusk seven days a week, with little food or water, and no pay. He had been kept in a long shed, had to sleep on the dirt with everyone else, and they washed from buckets of water. For toilets, they had to use holes that were dug inside the shed, and the shed stunk until they opened the doors at first light. He got an opportunity to run one day when there was a commotion at the other end of the field they were working, so he took it. He didn't know what happened to those he left behind, and he'd always felt guilty about running.

The following Sunday, Ramone made a call from a public pay phone to the police, to tell them about the farm. Unfortunately, in his haste not to be kept on the phone long, he failed to give the name of the farm or its address.

The case was passed to Olivia, and it was still not certain if the traced call was a hoax or not. Olivia had one of her young agents with a motorcycle, go and take a look around the fields, listen to the chatter that was going on, especially with the truckers, and to report in if any of the fields were being picked on a Sunday. It took quite a while, and she was already thinking of bringing the agent back to work on another case, when he called with some news. A trucker he'd got pally with at a truck stop, had told him how one farm was keeping him very busy. Load after load was being shipped by the trucks to the retailers, far more than any other farm. Mondays especially were the busiest, and they even had to call in extra trucks. It was almost as if the farm had picked on Sunday as well as Saturday. Olivia told him to go to the farm, to stay out of sight, do some surveillance, and see if anything was amiss. Then after he'd taken a look, call back in with what he'd seen.

Two days later, all excited, the young agent called in and related the same story as the anonymous caller had, but with the name of the farm and the location. Olivia congratulated him, told him what a good job he'd done, and to wait there for further instructions.

It was a huge farm, and after Olivia and her team had seen it on google and put the map of the farm on the case board, she knew that if they just went down the long dirt road to the farm, everybody would be running in all directions, and they'd be lucky to apprehend even one of them. Other agencies would need to help, and at least a couple of helicopters from Stockton police to keep an eye on the runners.

With a warrant in hand, Olivia and her team moved in, some in regular cars, others in ATV's and on motorcycles. As Olivia headed down the dirt road to the farmhouse, other agents who had got in place beforehand, were already apprehending the armed men in high chairs, with help from overhead. The pickers were being gathered together and were heading back to the barn. The farmer himself tried to escape by taking his tractor, but one of the helicopters stopped him, and after he began to run on foot, he was quickly chased down by a leaner and much quicker agent.

The shed was repulsive. Olivia had come across a lot of dead bodies in various degrees of decay, but this was awful. With the smell of dirty bodies, their sweat, clothing, mixed in with the old hay they slept on, and portable toilets that probably hadn't been replaced for weeks, she almost gagged. Some of the regular police actually did so, running back outside with hands covering their mouths.

The pickers were in a terrible state. Malnourished, many diseased, sunburnt, thin as rakes, hollow cheeked, sores on their hands and feet that hadn't had any treatment, skins bitten by flies, teeth rotting because they hadn't been given brushes or toothpaste, and they all stunk to high heaven. Olivia had to bring in a medical team who set up a triage, and soon it looked like a first aid camp for soldiers in battle. All the while, the farmer sat on a chair, handcuffed, watched by two agents who wanted to throttle him, feeling sorry for himself because he'd been caught.

He said later, with his lawyer in attendance and attempting to get a deal, that he only leased the pickers because it made financial sense. After renting them and paying for security, it still worked out much cheaper than hiring the regular pickers, and his new pickers even worked on Sundays rather than go to church like the others always did. The farmer didn't think he'd done anything wrong. In his own mind, he'd paid for the labor, fed them and kept them sheltered, and did what any American was supposed to do. Make money.

As none of the children or even the adults had been sexually exploited by him, he wouldn't get a long prison term and the pickers would be escorted back to Mexico. Olivia knew that, was sickened by it, but all she could do was catch them, and send them to court. But at least the farmer gave up his contact for the lease of the pickers. That was a very bad decision he made but Olivia had no intention of telling him that. He could deal with the repercussions himself.

CHAPTER 39

A couple of weeks later, it was a Friday night and Olivia had made it home, had dinner with her family, and had read a story to her girls before they went to sleep.

Back downstairs, in her comfy's now she was home, she was having a glass of wine with Kyle, just relaxing, her mind totally ignoring the television that was still on as she snuggled up to her husband.

"I've been thinking," she said.

"Uh oh, I hate those words," replied Kyle.

"Just listen oaf. I've been thinking we should take a vacation. A week or two somewhere, just you, me, and the girls. I've got some time coming, so what do you think?"

"I think it's a great idea. My work is very flexible and if you tell me when, I can prepare and get ahead. But what about you, it's never ending for you."

"I know, but I need a break from it. My team are very capable of handling things in my absence, so a week or so somewhere would be perfect. I'd come back all refreshed to catch more of these awful people who have no consideration for anyone but their own. So how about it honey. Do you want to spend some quality time with your loving wife?"

"I do. Very much so. We miss you around here. Do you still like your job?"

Olivia thought for a moment as she took a drink of her wine.

"Yes I do. I love my job and I'm glad I'm in this branch of the FBI rather than one of the others. It does seem never ending sometimes, but the people we catch need to pay for what they do. But finding these kids and stopping their pain is so rewarding. So where shall we go?"

"How about Maui?" Replied Kyle with a broad smile. "Sun, sea, sand, sex, and most importantly, golf!"

"Can we afford it?"

"I think so. So what do you think?"

"I think we should book it before we find an excuse not to go. Do you really have to play golf?"

"Just once or twice. I've always wanted to play there, and I could go very early in the morning before anyone wakes up."

"Okay, but what about the sex? Do you think we need to practice doing it quietly?" She teased.

"Maybe, we'll start tonight. But before I ravage you," he smiled, "I need you to come and look at something out back."

Kyle got up and put down his glass. Olivia wondered what his little secret was as she too got up and put down her glass.

"It's not another set of golf clubs is it?" She asked, following him outside to the garden shed.

Kyle ignored the question. Instead, he opened the shed door, put the light on, then stood back as Olivia approached and then looked inside.

"Oh my God, they're gorgeous. How did you know, and why two?" She asked, getting to her knees.

"Because they'll fight over one, so I thought why not one each. They've been bugging me for ages and it seems, you as well. If I have to look after one, it may as well be two, and they'll be company for each other."

"What kind are they? Where did you get them from?"

"They're Labrador retrievers. I can take them back if you don't want them. A golf buddy offered them to me."

"Don't you dare. They're adorable," Olivia giggled, as both puppies licked her as she scooped both bundles of fur into her arms on the floor. "Have they been spayed?"

"Just the other day. So what do you want to do?"

"What will we do with them if we go to Maui?"

"I'm sure my parents will look after them. You know how much they like dogs."

"Have the girls seen them yet?"

"No. I wanted you to see them first, to see what you thought or if I should take them back. They'll still find a good home to go to."

"So are these sisters as well?"

"Yes. They're from the same litter and their mother is so gentle."

Olivia got up with one of the puppies in her arms, so happy and carefree for once.

"I think we need to wake up the girls. I'll race you there!"

She ran back to the house as Kyle picked up the sister, turned off the light, closed the door to the shed, then ran after Olivia. He wondered what he'd got himself into as he chased her upstairs, both of them yelling at the girls to wake up as they had a big surprise for them.

AFTERWORD

Slavery isn't dead. It's thriving under its new name, Human Trafficking. Worldwide, 35 to 50 Billion Dollars a year is being earned by those who run the human trafficking networks.

Conservative estimates say almost 2 million people a year are trafficked, including around 100,000 people in the U.S.

75% of those that are trafficked are female, and 80% of the victims are forced into the sex trade. The rest are used for forced labor in sweat shops, farms, in regular homes, and for organ removal.

Only one in every hundred of those who are trafficked are ever rescued, and the life expectancy of a child prostitute, once she or he has been forced into the business, is 7 years.

If you wish to learn more about this truly awful trade, or to help in some way, then please visit one or more of the following websites:

www.fbi.gov
www.ice.gov/human-trafficking/
www.humantrafficking.org
www.polarisproject.org
www.chennaichildren.com

OTHER NOVELS BY THE AUTHOR

STONEBRIDGE MANOR

Lady Baldwin loves the wealth, her huge country mansion, homes in London and the Caribbean that her husband, Lord Baldwin, has provided for her.

Being beautiful and sexy, she is bored of her husband and his aristocratic friends, much preferring her show business friends from London. They are far more exciting and interesting.

She also likes to control and manipulate everyone around her purely for her own amusement. Not to mention being sexually adventurous with her men friends, even if they are in relationships with others.

When Lady Baldwin is found dead after a tempestuous weekend gathering, it seems that everyone is a suspect as everyone had a motive to kill her.

An old fashioned whodunit but set in 1994, this book will keep you guessing almost to the last page.

PROSPECTS

Alec and George are two brothers who live in the San Francisco area. Alec in the City, and George on the family farm just across the Bay Bridge. Both are rich, very intelligent, but Alec is much more handsome than his younger brother.

Alec has been dreaming of killing beautiful women for a long time, purely because he doesn't want another man to be able to enjoy them in the way he has. He wants to be their last good memory. Problem is, he finds that he doesn't like to do the kill.

That's where George steps in. Working on the sheep farm has gotten him used to taking life, and being a former rapist, he can't resist spending his own time with Alec's gorgeous young women.

Will they get away before Detective Garcia finds some evidence against them?

This novel highlights the huge problem of missing people, especially the young women, who literally fall off the face of the earth for no apparent reason. If there is no evidence to suggest otherwise, then there is very little the police can do.

CONSEQUENCES

All through school and into his working days, James was bullied and mistreated. The schools didn't protect him, and the adults he worked with were just glad it was he and not them that was always being yelled at.

Preferably, James would like all his persecutors to apologize to him, but if not, they have to face the Consequences of their actions.

Believing that he's alone in the world, James doesn't worry about what might happen to him after ruthlessly dealing with a couple of his tormentors, but he begins to change after meeting up with Alice. She was also mistreated, and James discovers that there are also millions more who need assistance, or just someone to listen to their stories.

James gets even with his own bullies, and unbeknown to Alice, he deals with her main one as well. Setting up a website to help the others, he steps in personally for a couple of victims, and finds he has a purpose in life.

This story was inspired by my grandson Bryce, who is bullied and not protected in his school. He is bullied because he's autistic.

ABOUT THE AUTHOR

Peter C. Bradbury was raised in a small, former cotton mill town, called Shaw, which is located North East of Manchester, in England.

After leaving school early, Peter did a lot of work in hotels and restaurants around the coast of England, Wales, and Jersey, before finally, at the ripe age of thirty, he trained to be a butler.

After working for Judges, and titled individuals in England, in 1994 he travelled to California for the World Cup, and on the last night of his vacation met his future wife, Debbie.

He moved to California at the end of that same year, then took his new family to Dallas, Texas where he worked as a butler for a family there. It was while in Dallas that he started Stonebridge Manor, but he didn't finish it until he found himself out of work, back in California, during the recession.

Still married to Debbie, Peter enjoys writing but no matter the subject, he wants to entertain his readers and keep them turning the pages.

52421251R00167

Made in the USA
Charleston, SC
18 February 2016